THE FATTENING HUT

The Fattening Hut

PAT LOWERY COLLINS

Houghton Mifflin Company

Boston 2003

ACKNOWLEDGEMENTS

I wish to express grateful thanks to my friends who kept me going on this book with the often repeated mantra "Just keep writing" and who read the drafts, shared their insights, and gave me encouragement all along the way. Among these flesh and blood muses, writers themselves, were Suzanne Freeman, Anita Riggio, and Lenice Strohmeier. Thanks also to my editor, Margaret Raymo, whose keen perception and editorial skill I've learned to trust completely.

www.houghtonmifflinbooks.com

The text of this book is set in 11-point Dante.

Library of Congress Cataloging-in-Publication Data
Collins, Pat Lowery.
The fattening hut / Pat Lowery Collins.
p. cm.
Summary: A teenage girl living on a tropical island runs away to escape her tribe's customs of arranged marriages and female genital mutilation.
ISBN 0-618-30955-1
[1. Runaways—Fiction. 2. Female circumcision—Fiction. 3. Sex role—Fiction. 4. Islands—Fiction. 5. Tropics—Fiction.] I. Title.
PZ7.C68353Fat 2003   [Fic—]dc21   2002151923

Manufactured in the United States of America
MP 10 9 8 7 6 5 4 3 2 1

For all the girls and women in the world who have no voice

Miduna is clicking like a beetle in her sleep
and making little snorts and wheezes
that pinch the dark. The noise
when she thrashes on the palm leaves
is a loud annoying rustle.
But at least I am not by myself in here.
Aman was the only one within
her father's fattening hut for many weeks.
He took her out the minute
her mother reported to the neighbors
how her belly was now resting on her thighs
when she sat cross-legged.
"Good work," Aman tells me her mother exclaimed
as she lay her hand upon her head like a blessing.
"You have made us proud."
Aman beams with pleasure when she tells me,
her face so round her smile dissolves
before it pushes out her cheeks.
Her whole family is quite proud of her.
In just four months
she has become as solid and plump
as her much older sister.
Her breasts now rise
like melons on the vine.
"You will love it, Helen," she said

upon the day she left the fattening hut.
"Everything you like to eat.
And all you want—rice, yams, beans,
pigeon peas with guinea corn,
your favorite ways for kingfish
and red snapper. Coconut pudding, too.
The whole day long!"
I do like yams and rice, the way my mother
and the other women make them.
Aunt Margaret, my father's sister,
cooks them much too long,
cooks everything too long.
I think that she will not be asked to help,
for she is not included in such things.
But I would try to eat
her tasteless plantains and all else
if only she would be included.
The first day in the hut has gone by slowly,
even though my sister Miduna
came to stay during the second meal.
She is already married with a baby
who stays close to her
so he can nurse all through the day
while she grows even fatter.
Miduna spends most
of the time between his feedings
in eating bowls and plates of food
the women have prepared. If she leaves
just a little, all the women are upset.

They say a healthy mother
has to eat as much as possible.
It is her first child and a time for her to spend
in learning how to care for him as well.
When she is fat enough and sure of what
to do for him, she will leave, too.
But I don't like to think of that,
of being all alone in here,
even though Miduna snores.
I have never slept
within a room alone before,
and this room
has been empty for so long
that it feels full of ghosts.
Three sisters have been shut in here
before Miduna and myself. Maybe
it is the ghosts of each young girl.
I remember peeking in at them and wondering
if I could ever sit so still so long.
They seemed to be much larger versions
of our household god, Hamani,
who sits upon his legs within his niche
above the candle fire, cheeks and belly
rosy and as round as a ripe peach.
Sometimes I hid in here with Suba,
the youngest girl within our family,
one year younger than myself.
But even then I knew we did invade
a sacred place, and Father always

shooed us out in anger
when he discovered us inside.
It is a larger hut than most,
with walls of daub and wattle
washed white inside. It sits
directly on the ground
to keep the women serving here
from climbing up and down into the trees
where many other dwellings rest.
There is an opening high at the top
where I can just make out some twisted branches
and a very tiny square of blue.
The walls slope outward from this opening
and then sweep down like petals
from the center of a giant flower.
The fire's smoke drifts up and out into the trees.
There is a pleasant smell of simmering earth
and of the sweet oaxa burned
to calm the room's inhabitants.
Around the hearth, there is much space
in which to place a mat or many mats
whenever there's a need.
I never looked expectantly
to spending time here
like Aman did in her own father's hut.
I did not dream of it like cousin Ene,
who entered with such eager pleasure
when she was only twelve years old.
At the time I was quite young

but wondered afterward
why no one told me when she did emerge
and why I never saw her since that time.
Our mother said that Ene's husband
took her far away. What husband, and how far?
Why did she never bring her babies back?
I had prayed that I would not
be shut in here so soon.
Miduna was sixteen years old
before her fattening,
while I am only fourteen and unready.
I told them this, but no one listened.
"You reached your moonflow long ago," Miduna said,
as if the onset of my bleeding time
means that I should have been here earlier.
They didn't listen even when Aunt Margaret cried
and made a fist right in my father's face.
"Just look at you," my mother told her cruelly.
It was not something that I had not heard before.
"No husband. No children of your own.
Do we want this for our Helen?"
"She runs too much with that Ashani boy,"
my father said, "and acts just like a boy herself.
We need to slow her down, to feed her things
that cause a girl to blossom,
or, you soon will see, no man will look at her."
Ashani looks at me, I could have told him.
But, of course, a daughter
does not speak so to a father.

And, I thought, *Ashani is not ready yet*
to marry anyone. We have been friends
for all the years I can remember.
Our mothers worked together
as we played beneath their busy feet.
Later they trusted us to roam
while in an elder sister's care
as if we were obedient pets
that would undoubtedly return.
So often, Suba was content to stay behind.
I do not know a time, however,
when I did not follow
close behind Ashani
except this one,
this long day without a tree to climb
or field to run through, and no caves
or nests of pelicans to search.
Our days of play upon this island
fill my mind with colors and bright light
that break most happily into this darkened room.
They say the island's shape is like a kingfish,
fat behind the gills and narrow at the tail.
Ashani knows each turn and swell of it,
for, as a boy, he was encouraged to explore.
I had to sneak away to follow him,
or wait until all members of my family
were engaged in other things
so I could disappear,
as I have done so many times,

to learn the island's secrets. In my mind's eye,
it shimmers like the scales upon a fish,
for there is sun here almost every day
and rain enough to make the flowers glisten
as they grow both beautiful and large.
Miduna's voice breaks suddenly
into my thoughts
and makes me painfully aware
that I have sat upon this mat
so long my muscles burn.
"When you are fatter," she instructs me,
"you will have a cushion for your legs,
which are now skinny as a hen's. You'll see.
I was so skinny, just like you. Remember?"
I do remember, for it was not long ago.
Where did that jumping, running sister go?
The air seems to have swallowed her.

My mother comes to check the baby
in the middle of the night. I keep
my eyes closed as she passes my pandanu mat
and pats my cheek with her plump hand.
I think she is quite happy
that her next-to-youngest girl,
the wildest one, is now within the hut at last.
I think she must feel more content.
I reach beneath my covering
to run my hand along
the stiff spines of the books

Aunt Margaret bundled in my clothing pack.
I do not dare to take them out
during the time Miduna is awake
and all the women come and go.
Right now there is such dim light
from the little fire. Not enough
to read by. No woman ever reads in here,
or anywhere. But I will. I will find a way.

Mother says that if the English people
had not come here
when Aunt Margaret was a child,
to study all our customs and our ways,
and if they had not kept a school
upon the island for a time,
for girls as well as boys,
she would not have this trouble with me now.
There were some poets in the group
who wished, they said, to use their words
"to let the light into the dark."
This seemed an insult to the elders here.
Yet as unwelcome as the strangers were,
they stayed until my aunt
was a young woman
and had grown so close to one kind lady
that she took her English name
and would not answer to her tribal one.
In fact, as mother's children came along,
Aunt Margaret tried to teach us all to read.

I had already learned
before our father burned up all the books
that he could find
which had no use within the school for boys.
Miduna can remember how
he used to call upon Hamani in his prayers
and promise reparation
for the fact he had allowed our mother
to confer on me one of the poet's names.
Whenever he would find me reading books
he would storm out
and go in search of our aunt Margaret
just to bellow right into her face
that her fine English name
would never serve her well.
Once he slapped her, in his anger,
raising welts like tiny reddened snakes.
After that, Aunt Margaret moved
out of her hut
and to the very smallest village
all the way across the island.
She gave to me, in secret,
a small parcel of the books
that she had somehow kept.
I struggle now with some of them.
They speak of things and places
I have never heard about or seen.
They have small pictures
of pale people in strange clothing.

One talks about a woman named Amelia who can fly.
I believe it is not true. But imagine!
Think what it would be
to skim so high above the ground
just like pelicans or grouse.
I have a picture of it in my head.
If I should never open up the books again,
I have so many pictures in my head
from all the words I have already read.
Father cannot take these away.

Sleep comes to me as I am flying like Amelia.
When I open up my eyes,
the sun is flooding through the doorway,
and Usanna, the quiet mother
of Miduna's husband, Dar,
is blocking out a little of its light.
She is not as large a woman as our mother,
for which she does lament from time to time.
Her sons are grown men
and there are but two of them.
"A pity," says our mother
when she speaks of it at all.
She feels great pity for Usanna
but is happy for her own high standing in the tribe.
Our mother has been blest
with sons and daughters both.
She is a large warm mother
with a deep and comfortable lap

and arms that rest most heavily upon us.
I must pull and pull on them
to get her up from where she sits.
"It is a lesson for you, Helen," Mother says
when speaking of Usanna. "She went
into the fattening hut too late
and came out much too soon."
No doubt that is the other reason
for my being sent in here so early.
I regret this very much but can do nothing
but attempt to be a daughter who is good.
I think I will succeed, but when the first meal
of the day arrives, I cannot eat at all. One bite
of the immense dish of galassa
that is placed before me,
runny with clear juice,
and a pain sinks deep into
the very middle of myself.
I must double over just to bear it.
"What is the matter?" asks Miduna.
I cough and sputter.
"There is something wrong with the galassa."
She reaches over me to take a bite
and runs her tongue along her lips.
"Not at all," she says. "It is delicious."
Just looking at it causes
such a bitter rush into my throat,
I retch into the basket by the door.
"You must be sick," says Mother

when she comes to get the bowl.
Yet even as she takes it from me,
my stomach starts to settle like a rippling lake
and in just minutes it is absolutely still.
"I do not understand," says Miduna.
"You love galassa."
I do not understand it either.
It is one
of all the many things
I do not understand.

2

I am so sound asleep when Mother comes
with the first meal of the day
she has to shake me.
"How can you be this tired
when you do not do a thing?" she asks.
It puzzles me as well. I feel
just like a stone fused with the earth,
or else a beast too large
to lift itself on its own haunches. Perhaps
I have grown fat in just one night
and will be told that I may leave here
sooner than I thought. Miduna laughs
when I sit up to better see myself,
holding one arm and then a leg up to the light.
"What can you be expecting, little cayawolf?"
She has called me this
since I was just a howling infant,
and she says I still make wild and whimpering sounds
within my sleep. "Those who do not eat
will turn to skin and bone,
then crumble into dust and blow away."
"She *will* eat," says our mother when she comes again.
She puts a serving of warm millet down in front of me,
covered with a crust of honey and thick cream.
The cream is warm. "Here."

She hands me my own wooden spoon,
the one that I have used since I was small.
The birds upon the handle
were carved there by my older brother Nam.
"It will be just as if you sit about the family table."
I miss my brothers and the gentle teasing
that has always been a part of life at home.
I miss my sister Suba,
the frog faces she would make
when Father turned away,
to make me laugh.
The spoon is so familiar
that at first the millet goes down easily.
"Don't hurry so," cautions Miduna.
"You will make yourself get sick again."
I try to eat more slowly,
tasting all the blossoms in the honey,
feeling the smooth cream
as it slips pleasantly along my throat.
"Praise Ossada," says our mother, giving thanks,
"you are no longer sick."
Father does not permit Ossada's fetish
in the hut or near the altar to Hamani.
So mother keeps it with her at all times,
tucked tightly in the wide sash
that is called a *dabbi*. Mother's dabbi
is quite wide and colorful,
respecting both her size and the large number
of children she has born.

She puts her bouncy hand against my
forehead. "If there had been a fever,
you could not have stayed here with Miduna."
How does one get this fever? Is it hovering
where I can gather it within my hands?
If I sleep but little, will it come to me?
It would be such an easy way
to get away from here.
Miduna nurses George and eats at the same time.
It is a strange sight as her hand
goes back and forth to her own mouth
above the sucking baby.
She says the eating helps to make more milk.
We were surprised she gave
her firstborn child the name
of some fine English king.
Father, of course, was angry
and would no doubt
have ordered that
the child must be renamed
if Miduna hadn't always been the docile one,
the one who did whatever she was told.
"I would expect this from our Helen, or even
from your little sister Suba," he told her, "but not from you."
I wonder at it still, why such a tiny disobedience
should have so much importance to her.
Is it the start of something,
or the last of what made her
defy Father in the first place?

Mother puts a pile of reeds beside Miduna,
some still slightly green.
"You will have much time in here to make
the baskets you will need within your household
and to teach our Helen, too," says Mother.
"Helen will soon need baskets of her own."
I can't imagine sitting in this place all day
and weaving baskets. Some say
that they will put a loom in here as well
for weaving cloth the way
the English women taught our mothers.
I do not plan to weave one thing.
But Miduna seems delighted.
"Look, Helen. All these lovely reeds!
And we didn't even have to harvest them ourselves!"
"I do not have a household," I tell her.
"I will never have a household!"
I have lost my appetite again
and feel so sluggish suddenly
I throw myself upon my mat and try to disappear.
"None of that, Helen," says Mother.
"You have not been put in here to dream.
Too many dreams will only court the Evil One."
Dreams from the Evil One are dark. My dreams
are full of colors and bright light.
They are all sky on top of sky. I ride the wind.
Mother pulls me by the shoulders so I stand
and then she winces when I yawn into her face.

"What will we do with you? A fine man like Esenu
will not settle for a skinny girl as wife,
or a lazy one who dreams."
Miduna looks up with surprise.
I am so startled that I cannot speak.
"Esenu," I finally stammer—the words eke from my lips
like something full of prickers—"Esenu is old."
Mother laughs. "Not old. A man of only thirty years.
And never married. Think of that!"
I do think of it. Who would want to marry him?
His head is shaped just like a spiny melon.
He has no hair except upon his hands,
and he has eyes that cross beneath dark, bushy hoods.
"He owns a fine farm," says our mother,
"and will take good care of you."
I have seen the care some husbands take of wives.
I would rather be a favorite cow.

Miduna cannot wait to tell this news
and flings it at her friend Emara
just as soon as she steps in the hut.
I experience the words before
they even come out of Miduna's lips.
I clamp my hand upon her mouth,
although she grabs it, tears it away and laughs.
"You will never guess the husband
they have picked for this one,"
she says, pointing right at me.
"I know," says Emara.

"The whole village knows."

"Already?" says Miduna, disappointed

not to be the one to tell.

"Esenu has spread the news himself. He is

so delighted that he even smiles sometimes."

I cannot imagine any smile on Esenu

and am ashamed to be the one to put it on his face.

I want to hide away somewhere,

but Emara seems so genuinely pleased for me.

"He is a lazy, quiet man, Helen," she says.

"Once he gets used to having you as wife,

he will go back to spending all his days around the cows.

You wait and see. A husband like that

is much better than the kind who sits

upon the doorstep and is always in the way."

I do not want to take care of a quiet, tired man.

I do not wish to do for him the things a wife must do.

"I will not marry him," I say.

Mother is no longer in the hut, so I can safely say it.

Emara and Miduna are both shocked, however.

"You will do what Father tells you," says Miduna.

"It is a woman's duty."

"Why?" I ask.

There is bewilderment upon their faces.

"It is tradition," says Emara.

"The law," says Miduna. "The law of the tribe.

What woman chooses her own husband?

None of us is wise enough."

"Why?" I ask again. "I have read stories

in which people choose each other."
"In books!" says Miduna. "There is the trouble.
Father was quite right to burn the ones we had."
"What are these books?" Emara asks.
"Where is the place where people choose
each other? How far away?"
"It must be very far," I say,
"or others here would know of it."
I turn and lie upon my stomach,
my face crushed down into the mat.
What is the use?
Emara and Miduna can do nothing for me,
even if they really wanted to.
Emara's husband is gruff and demanding;
Miduna's husband, Dar, is so young he clings to her
as if she were the sun
and is as needy as a fussy child.
Neither woman would complain.
They are good women. This is what
it must mean to be good.
Mother is so good as well.
Ossada,
what am I?

3

I am all turned around. During the day
I cannot keep a dull and heavy sleepiness away;
at night my eyes are wide. They try
to penetrate the shadows.
What can I hope to see there?
The fire gives off light enough
so that Miduna does not nurse in darkness.
Soon after she has put the baby down,
she falls into a deep and snorting sleep.
Folds of her body swell
over the mat and push against me.
In the dark I try to trace
my slender jumping sister
in the fuller shape that she inhabits now.
I try to call it forth by whispering
an incantation from
the growing-season celebration for Ossada
and softly sing, "Spring up, Miduna."
I even take her hands to lift her, but she doesn't stir.
If we could really run away from here,
where would we go?
I have no power over who she was
or is now. A tiny baby has more claim.
The women are all telling me
with words and without sound

that I have no power even over
what I think of as myself.
Yet in the dark I sense it,
this power and this knowledge of the one I am.
It is kindled by something
that lives so deep
I wonder if Ossada is the one
to make me so aware of it.
Why has she not informed
the others of this need?
Why does each one go willingly
into a life arranged by those
who seem to know them not at all?

My aunt arrives at daybreak,
before anyone has brought our breakfast.
She must have started very early
from her hut, while it was dark.
She sighs as she holds up her walking stick
to part the reeds that fill the doorway.
Her free arm holds a bulky package
wrapped in skins.
"Such a long walk!" she exclaims,
collapsing onto one end of my mat
and crossing her long legs in front of her.
Her black hair flares with silver rivers,
but her face looks young
and vibrant as a wild brown orchid
in the clear light of the morning.

Her cheekbones cradle large soft eyes
as blue as sky or water.
When she hugs me,
there is little flesh to rest against,
and yet her touch is comforting and gentle.
Except for my dark eyes, I am like her, they say,
and I am proud to be.
She thrusts her package down into my lap.
Miduna turns and mumbles something, half asleep.
She was up with George, just hours earlier
and ever since I have been wide-awake.
"So early," are the words I think she says,
but her eyes don't open, and she turns away.
"Hurry," whispers Aunt Margaret.
"Before your mother comes."
I unwrap the bulky package, knowing well
it is not any kind of food. Inside
are three worn books I have not seen before.
"Hide them," says Aunt Margaret.
She does not need to tell me this.
Without looking at the pictures on the front,
I bury them beneath my covering,
with all the other books.
"I thought there were no more," I say,
"that father had destroyed them all."
"My brother is not clever," is her answer.
I am grateful that she feeds me in these ways
the others cannot understand. I hug her long and hard.
"You are still just a twig," she says,

showing her large, even teeth.

Her fingers circle my thin wrists.

"They have not made you mountainous just yet."

"And it will not be soon," I tell her, "for I cannot eat."

"So I have heard. Your father storms about, they say,

directing what to cook and how to make you keep it down.

He claims he'll send the Healer in a day or two,

that time is being wasted.

I dare not show my face.

If he should find me here, this time

he might well chase me off the cliff unto my death."

Her laugh is somber.

"He cannot choose a hut more distant

or a village smaller

than the one which I inhabit now."

"Do not go," I plead.

"I will come again."

She smoothes my hair

and kisses me between the eyes.

The reeds rush just like water

as she passes through them and is gone.

After a while of wishing

that she could have stayed,

I slip out one slim book

to see the title, *Ladies of the Air.*

I have read a book

about some English ladies once before,

in which they go about to parties

and in search of men to marry.

I flip the pages. There are pictures here
of women in strange costumes with tight hats,
big shiny circles around each eye
that meet across the nose.
They sit in large stiff birds and wave to me.
Do these fine ladies ride the birds into the air
the way Amelia does?
How wonderful it would be!
I picture Aunt Margaret in a hat like this,
her long hair blowing from beneath it.
I see her rising up into the sky.
Once I saw a bird like the ones pictured here.
I believe it is still there, inside the island,
in a place where I, and Ashani, too,
have been instructed not to go.
Ashani has been almost everywhere, however.
It would not be a possibility
for him to lose his way.
"If you had been allowed to roam the island as I have,"
Ashani told me once, "you
would know all its secrets, too."
"Or even more!" I answered him.
He smiled. "Perhaps."
When I am with him I know this,
that it is safer than our hearth.
The day I told him of Amelia,
he told me of the giant bird,
what this book calls an aeroplane.
I could not wait to see it

and was astonished when I did.
The beak of the poor broken thing
was driven far into the earth.
The wings had seared right through three palms.
But it had never truly been alive, this bird.
There was no heart to it. I think the heart
must be within the one who sits
upon the seat behind the wings.
Lady Bailey, pictured here within the book,
is such a heart,
and Lady Heath. There is someone
called Duchess in a shiny coat.
Their strange and careful dress, the way they pose,
I think they must be getting ready for
some kind of ceremony of the air.
I hold the book against me
with the pages open while I picture it
and how Ashani says that he will learn to fly
this aeroplane one day. He always
does the things he plans. I wonder
if this skill will take him long to learn.
I hear a scraping sound and hide the book.
It may be someone coming
with the first meal of the day.
A pebble bounces at my feet,
and I look up to see the piece of tree and sky
and then a face, Ashani's face, grinning at me.
How did he climb so high?
I see his hand upon a branch

but cannot guess his means
of scaling the hut's sloping sides.
I should have known that he would find a way,
but if the others should discover him
the punishment will be severe.
I wave my arms at him to go away,
yet feel a smile upon my face that tells him, *Stay.*
I stand and smile and raise my hands above my head.
Oh, stay, Ashani, stay.
Please pull me quickly through the opening
and out into the trees and then beyond . . . beyond.

Someone is banging pots and screeching.
There is a scuffle near the door
as Mother pushes through the doorway
with a kettle on each hip.
Her head cloth is unraveling,
but she takes the kettles to the fire carefully,
huffing as if the effort
is much more than she can bear.
"That crazy boy," she says and looks at me.
"What does he think, lurking about so early,
as if at any moment you'll be running out to play,
as if you both were children still.
Shanana should keep better watch upon her only son."
"You did not frighten him away?"
"I did my best."
She heaves herself upon the low stool by the door,
unwrapping her head cloth
and letting colors stream as it unfolds;
her curly hair is glistening with sweat.
She raises her large body so she stands
and breathes most heavily
while lining up the bowls
that she begins to fill.
Today the porridge floats
in milk of coconut with chopped papaya.

Nanina carries in a steaming tray of pana,

the sweetness of it drifting all about the room.

It is her specialty and she is smug with pride.

"No one makes pana quite like you," says Mother.

Nanina smiles, displaying teeth as dark as earth.

"It is my blessing."

This is the proper thing for her to say, and Mother nods.

Emara reappears with crescents

of cantabu melon dripping rich red juice.

"I dare you not to eat breakfast this morning," she proclaims.

"There's nothing here that you don't like."

It's true, and I begin to feel a twinge of hunger.

It travels steadily right to the place

where I was severed from my birth cord.

I reach up for a melon crescent, eager for a juicy bite.

Emara smiles and Mother

quickly puts a bowl of porridge in my lap.

The smell of coconut is strong and sweet.

I try a spoonful, and it slips

behind the melon down my throat,

which suddenly begins to close.

I have to swallow hard

so I won't sputter back

what I have chewed already.

I cough and choke until

Mother's face twists up into a scowl.

"What is it now?" she asks,

as if I play a trick.

"When you began to eat you seemed just fine."

She and Miduna exchange looks so quizzical
I feel as if I must be tricking them
in some unknowing way.
I try once more and gag again.
This second try makes Mother
angrier than ever.
She leans over me with difficulty,
grasping my two shoulders with stout hands,
too weak to pull me up. I help by rising
by my own strength, even though
I have a notion of what will occur.
Her eyes on mine,
she slaps me hard upon the cheek.
A flood of hot tears shames me in her sight,
although her eyes are wet and red-rimmed, too,
as if she has been crying for some time.
"Your fattening," she says quite firmly,
"is too important to be spoiled by silly games.
Your father has begun
to question me both day and night.
I cannot tell him that you still refuse to eat."
"I do not refuse," I say.
I try again between my sobs.
I take the smallest spoonfuls, slowly.
At first they also stick within my throat,
but then slide down and soon become
a burning wad inside my chest.
Mother must be made to know
I do not mean to disobey.

Until a little of the food within the bowl
is eaten in this way, she stands and watches me.
She strokes the stinging place upon my cheek
where I still feel her open hand.
"It is your future, Helen," she says quietly.
"You must become a woman soon or Esenu
will travel from this island
to find another bride."
"There are not many choices here," my sister says.
"More reason why you must grow fat.
The tribe will suffer if you do not,
and you will have no future. None at all.
No one to care for you. No children of your own.
Your elders will not be revered in their old age."
I never have heard talk before
of seeking brides from other places.
Where are these places?
How would a man like Esenu
know where to look?
How would he have the strength
to paddle in a boat?
The only boats along the shore
are carved from trees
and are the width of one.
The men go just a little ways to fish.
They go in groups and never travel far.
Sometimes they carry salt blocks
to large vessels waiting
at a line between the sea and sky

as far away as anyone can see.
"It is only a threat," Miduna says
when I have asked all of my questions.
"It is a way to make you want to grow."
Grow up. Grow fat. They seem to be the same.

In books I have seen boats
with large white wings that catch the wind.
Aunt Margaret told me once
of how the boat came for the English long ago.
It had no wings, she said,
but three round chimneys on the top
that belched black smoke.
"The ship," she called it,
anchored in deep water, and the island people
took the English out
in our own little boats
so they could meet the ship and climb on board.
She wanted so to go along.
She felt, she said, as if something
inside of her would break in two.
These strangers had instructed and protected her
until she was no longer young enough to be a bride
but was instead both singled out
and shunned for her continued opposition
to the customs of the tribe.
"Perhaps they will come back,"
I told her once when she spoke so.
"To what?" she said.

"To people who refuse to learn,
who do not want to know of places
or of customs different from our own?
Have you never wondered
why our island has no name,
and why the tribe
would not let the English give it one?"
I did not know then that an island
as small as ours would have a name.
"Because," she said when I did not respond,
"without a name, it is not likely to be found."

5

All day I think of that long silver line against the sky
that none of us can see beyond.
Aunt Margaret said how
when the ship had sailed away
it curved, the smoke and all,
over the line and disappeared.
Is there perhaps a veil
the color of the sky that can be lifted
so that ships may slip beneath?
Is there a space that can be entered that is hidden
from the view of those on shore?
Of course, in here, in this dim room,
I cannot see the water or the line, the trees,
the people walking back and forth,
the children sifting sand from hand to hand.
I must rely on pictures in my mind.
Sometimes these pictures are as clear
as what I see with my own eyes; sometimes
they do not come at all.
All day I have tried hard
to eat so I will please them—
the women, those who come and go.
After they leave, I wait
until Miduna is asleep again
and then I retch into the basket by the door,

slipping out to bury
what I call up from my throat.
The food wells up until
it is a thing that I must rid my body of
or I will burst just like a fruit that is too ripe.
Perhaps Ossada is the one
who makes this plain to me.
I do not know.
Five days pass in this way,
and Mother is amazed
to find me thinner than before.
She takes Ossada's fetish from her dabbi
and then passes it across my eyes, my mouth,
and right above my heart,
chanting in the language of the tribe
and asking that the goddess
dwell within this hut
and cause the food to fill me
just as if I were a sacred vessel.
Her voice is tearful, and I feel ashamed.
She shakes her head
as though she cannot understand.
"Miduna," she says finally, "does not
our Helen eat each time you do?"
"Not each time. But I do watch to see
that she has something, and when I look again,
it is not there. Perhaps
she is too young for fattening.
Perhaps she should remain

a child a little longer."
"And be just like her aunt?
No husband and no children?"
Mother puts her face right next to mine and sneers.
"Think of that!"
Do I dare tell her that I have, so many times?

When Mother leaves, I pick up George
and cradle him the way Miduna does.
He roots against me, finds no milk, and starts to cry.
Miduna takes him from me,
puts him to her breast, and croons
until the squeak of sucking
makes a rhythm of its own.
She seems so happy and content
that I hesitate to ask her
what I need to know.
When no words have been spoken for some time
and all the silence presses us apart, I say,
"If you could not have children of your own,
what would you do?"
"You are a strange one, Helen.
Why would you think
a thing so awful and untrue?"
"It happens sometimes. Some women
in our tribe have long been barren."
"Well, praise Ossada, I am not of those."
She bends much closer and then whispers,
"You tempt the gods. You really do."

"I think I would not mind," I tell her.
"You cannot know that, Helen.
 You cannot know how empty you would feel."
"I could play with all your children
 and could help you care for them."
"Of course you could. But it would
 certainly not be the same."
"Or bring the babies from the womb, like Aunt Margaret."
"And take none of them away with you? How very sad."
"Or I might spend my time in dancing, like Orena.
 She is happy all the time."
"And has no judgment. None at all.
 She chases blowing things all day."
How do I tell her there are dreams in me
that must be given names, that there are
many, many things I need to learn and do?

A torrent of hot air, the heavy thud of feet,
a feathery rush, a chant so high
and piercing that we hold our ears!
The huge and horrifying Healer's mask
dips over me with an inhuman scowl.
Before I have a chance to move away,
it comes so close that I can smell
the berry stains upon the cheeks,
spoiled melon scent and smoke
that leaks from puffy lips. A cry
is barely held behind my teeth.
I cringe against Miduna

as she shields the baby with one hand
while two large rattles made of bone
are shaken up and down beside my head.
The long arms of the Healer
carry them along my body to my feet.
He backs away, the awful smell grows fainter,
yet the face is just as fierce.
The snaggleteeth are wooden
like the mask itself; his surprise arrival
meant to catch the Evil One off guard.
I feel unsteady and so cold
that I begin to shiver uncontrollably.
Miduna whispers, "It is only Toba."
Yet it is difficult to think of that
while eerie sounds
continue coming from behind the mask.
I try to calm myself, but as he dances
all around the hut, shaking rattles
in the places he can reach, I feel
a hot and burrowing fear.
He bends the little that he can
and chants another incantation
filled with words I do not understand.
When he approaches me
and puts one knobby hand upon my head,
my eyes become immovable, a scream
stays buried deep inside my chest.
His ghostly chants and brutish moans
have filled each space and crevice in the hut

before he lights a fire stick
and places it right next to me, beside the hearth,
then, at the door, removes the mask and grimaces.
He is so old the ridges in his cheeks bunch up
and cross each other;
his cloudy pupils swim up to the light
and are more fearful than the mask.
I shudder as I think of his new wife, Aleda,
who has been Miduna's friend forever
though not a wife for very long.
What I really wish to know from her
is something I can never ask:
how one so very young can stay so merry
answering to one as old and stooped
as Toba has become
and to his other wives as well.
As if he has heard my thought, his face
becomes expressionless, the rattles quiet.
He turns his bent and decorated back to us
and sweeps away. My eyes
stay open all the night. I do not sleep.

Mother must read minds,
because it is Aleda whom she sends us
in the morning with our breakfast.
Aleda makes us laugh. It is her way,
and we are overjoyed to see her.
She whips the cloth away
from what she carries

as if uncovering a special offering.
She sings songs of her own making
as she ladles fruit with honey crusts
into large bowls that she
has built herself from island clay.
There are some wassa cakes,
light and sweet, and warm roasted nuts.
These are my favorite foods,
prepared in ways I like them best.
My stomach hums to think of them.
My own spoon dives right through the crusts
and scoops up melon, grapes, banana,
fruit that's shaped like stars.
"I knew they must be joking," she informs me,
crossing both her arms below her breasts.
She beams. "I told your mother this. I said to her,
'Would Helen turn down wassa cake?
Never, never!' It was, of course, exactly true."
I take a bite of one and feel its sweetness in my teeth.
It crunches pleasantly.
The second bite is not so sweet.
My throat begins to close once more,
and I begin to sense that I will choke.
Miduna pats me reassuringly upon the back.
She holds another bite of cake up to my lips.
I push her hand away.
"I know you want to help," I say,
"but I will only have to spit it back."
I hold my own hands to my throat,

which tightens up so much
that I can barely swallow.
My breath comes out in shallow bursts
as if I have been climbing a great hill.
Aleda is dismayed.
She jokes, "You want to shame me.
When I take this meal back to my hut,
they all will say, 'Aleda is no cook at all.
She cannot even please a little girl.'"
She means to tease,
but when she calls me "little girl"
something inside my throat is soothed.
My breath comes out more easily.
"Leave it all," Miduna tells Aleda
and takes a generous helping for herself.
"Perhaps a little later on
her appetite will reappear."
"If you do not finish it," Aleda says.
She smiles to see the food that she prepared
consumed so eagerly. She launches easily
into the gossip of the village
—what wives have quarreled,
who has been punished,
who will be next into the fattening hut,
what plans are being made
to celebrate the day that I emerge,
how many cows are being given for my dowry,
how Esenu has now begun to worry.
Miduna shushes Aleda

the minute that she says his name,
as though if we don't speak of him
we can pretend he isn't out there waiting.
But I can see his loathsome face
in every space between the words they say.
When Miduna is quite finished with Aleda's food,
she yawns, lies down upon her side,
and curls herself into a ball.
Aleda sighs. "That is right. Do not wait
until I go to fall asleep."
Miduna has a sleepy smile upon her lips.
"It helps the meal to blossom in the loins and breast,"
she says, as I have heard our mother say
so many times before. From looking at Miduna
I can see it's true. Each morsel that has passed
Miduna's lips must now be working hard
to make her even larger.
I sleep almost as much as she does,
but there is not enough inside of me
to make me bloom so.
As Aleda starts to leave
I put my hand upon her arm
and look into her face.
Except for fuller cheeks, she seems
no different from the girl
who has been close to us as Suba.
Her eyes ask what it is I want to say.
"What is it like?" I ask.
She knows exactly what I mean.

"He provides well for me.
 As Healer he is well revered."
"And much too old to father children."
"No," she says and smoothes the skirt
 of her danabo with both hands.
 The mound between her hips astounds me.
"It is his child, Helen." She does not smile.
"What more blessing could be wished for?"
 What more?
 There must be something more!

6

It is deep night
when we go softly from the hut
to bathe ourselves in tidal waters
lapping near the door.
It is the third time
we have been allowed to do so,
and Miduna watches me
as if she has been named my keeper.
The air is warm and heavy in the way
our island air is at this time.
The people in their huts up in the trees
are fast asleep. Some snore so loudly
they compete with the Zunabi birds
that caw into the tamarinds all night.
I leave my new danabo on dry sand
and lie barebacked upon the place
that has been dampened by the tide.
Miduna folds hers at the waist
and keeps it wrapped around her hips.
The sudden coolness calms;
all our round places shine in moonlight,
and I can see quite clearly
I am like a ghost
of who Miduna has become.
As she stands up

to bathe herself, splashing water
like bright handfuls of small flowers,
it is plain that she enjoys
her bounty of new flesh,
that she feels beautiful.
I run ahead and dive into a wave
so that the light will not fall down on me
but on the ocean crests.
I look back at the shore
and there is nothing moving there
except Miduna, with her head back,
her hair floating in the wind.
I search the trees for any sign
of someone watching
and at times I see twin tiny bursts of fire,
a pair of eyes belonging to
some animal that hunts by night.
Ashani must be sleeping,
as it is best he should.
The night is quiet
and the sky so wide with stars
I feel as free as a small girl again.
But then the baby's cry
pierces the stillness like an arrow.
In haste Miduna dries herself with bathing cloths
while calling to me as she ties a dry danabo.
For just an instant I have seen
a flash of her bare body
made silvery by starlight.

I need to ask.
"Why do you not swim naked as I do?
There is no one about."
She laughs as if I am a hopeless child.
"With womanhood comes modesty. You will see."
I do not want to see.
If it were not for George's need of her,
I would not hurry so. I feel
so melancholy at the thought
of going back inside the hut
that tears are running from my eyes.
It is quite clear Miduna has been told
she cannot leave me here alone,
that I cannot be trusted to return.
When she decides I'm taking longer than I should,
she scolds me shrilly
until I have to turn and follow her.
My sleeping mat feels damper than my skin,
but all I want to do is sleep, now.
The air inside the hut
is musty with trapped odors
from the unwashed cooking pots
and our own bodies. The fire sends
strange spirits leaping up the walls.
The baby sucks; Miduna
clucks soft sounds into the dark.

In the morning I hear noises
from the women long before I wake.

I feel the curl my body makes upon the mat,
the tightness of my eyelids to my cheek.
I have no wish to move or open up my eyes.
I have no wish to speak or try to smile.
Mother's laugh is loud.
The other women laugh as well
at something that Aleda says.
They rustle all about me,
setting up their dishes.
A foot brushes by my cheek;
another grazes my bare feet.
I pull the sleeping cover close about myself.
"She is awake," I hear our mother whisper.
She lifts her voice and says, "Helen,
you cannot burrow any longer there.
The moon has slipped back down into the sea."
"The sun rose like a fireball today," Aleda adds.
She shakes my shoulder.
"You would not believe the heat already,
even in the tamarind's shade."
What she says cannot be true,
or some fierce ocean god
has filled my bones with cold.
Aleda turns my chin up with her hand.
Her touch is warm.
I look into her pleasing face
and see small beads of sweat upon her head.
"You need to move about," she says.
"You need more of the food

which I have cooked for you."
I pull the covering around my shoulders and sit up.
Mother looks straight down at me,
and all the energy within her eyes
says we shall start again;
this is another day; she has not given up.
Aleda has prepared a plate of steaming sweet potato
wrapped in spicy oka leaves. There is a soft
and milky cheese that is her specialty.
It is so small a piece, so pale and white, to taste so large.
One bite and I feel much too full to speak.
Miduna has already asked for more
and eagerly consumed the contents
of each oka leaf upon her plate.
Her skin is shiny from the past night's salty bath.
The women are examining her baskets with respect.
They say fine words; she is already
choosing reeds to make another
as I look up through the roof and watch
the clouds form in the sky,
some dark enough for rain.
The wind is moaning like the voice of Toba.
"We must go home
and fasten down our mats and children," says Emara.
"The trees are bending down
and people will be blown
to places where they do not want to go.
Do you remember
how our Toba was once taken by the wind

into the smoking hut, head over his heels?"
The women laugh to think of the great Healer
at the mercy of the wind, of his bright feathers flying.
They scurry to collect whatever they have brought.
Some straighten up the hut and take away our refuse.
Jobs we would have been obliged to do for others
are performed for us, as if we are the honored guests.
"Enjoy your leisure and grow fat," Aleda tells us.
"Especially you!" She nudges me with one bare toe.
"I will put more wassa cake upon the coals
and bring it to you fresh this afternoon.
It will be much too sweet to turn away."
Fresh wassa cake is always wonderful.
Perhaps by afternoon my lips, my tongue,
my churning stomach will be able to enjoy it.
I stand to hug our mother as she starts to leave.
Her softness comforts me as it has always done,
but though she holds me tenderly as any of her children,
there is some sorrow in her grasp.
It is in just such ways
she has begun to send me from her.
The direction she has chosen for me
is one I cannot take, however,
and I badly want to tell her so,
to say there is a place
and I must find it for myself,
perhaps inside of me,
perhaps beyond the silver line.

7

The wind continues on into the night.
Miduna holds her ears so she can sleep.
I listen carefully as if its mouth
is telling secrets I must learn.
The trees scrape down the sides of our large hut
like claws of animals attracted to the fire.
I move as close as I can get to its unsteady light
and take another book out from my covering.
It is a book of many words set strangely on the page;
The curfew tolls the knell of parting day.
The lonely herd winds slowly o'er the lea.
I like the sound the words make, set together in this way,
though I do not know the thought they try to say.
Inside the pages of this book are yellow sheets
inscribed in my aunt Margaret's hand.
I have often seen the letters that she makes,
and also other notes and poems
from her fine English friends,
which she has saved for years.
These sheets do not appear to be a letter,
for they fold together like another book.
There is a title at the top: *An Island Story.*
Below this title is the name of *Margaret,*
then so many sentences in her careful hand:
When I was very little

there was a wise man called Medala
who could count back
to the beginning of his time here.
I did not listen hard enough
to all the things he said. Nor did the others.
What I did not hear or have forgotten
may have told us much.
What I have remembered tells a little.
In the caves before the cliffs
are pictures painted on the rock.
They are of men and women
and also of some fierce and unfamiliar animals.
The people look much smaller than our tribesmen.
They possess such short, thin bones;
the women little flesh.
Some of both men and women
hold long spears for hunting.
I do remember that Medala said
these pictures were of people
who had lived here since perhaps forever.
He said more people came here on a ship
from far across the sea, and he was one of them.
He and the others would have been called "slaves"
if they had reached the land to which they traveled.
A slave is someone, he was quick to tell me,
who is owned by someone else.
Like a wife? I wonder.
The ship had broken up upon the reef
around the far side of our island.

There had been some cows and sheep on board
that needed to be pulled with ropes
across the reef onto the land.
Some crates of chickens floated in or sank.
The seas were high and many
of both animals and people died.
It was so long ago, he said, that there
are few who can remember it.
He himself was a small boy,
separated from his parents at the place
of their departure from another land.
He recalled crying all the time and being beaten for it.
He recalled the cold for lack of clothing,
and getting warm by huddling next to strangers.
All people on this ship were not one color.
There were dark men selling others dark as they,
warm-skinned traders not as dark, and white ones, too.
Aunt Margaret has many times reminded me
the English on our island had been white,
but I was so young when they left I did not think
how there were lighter colors of the skin
than what I saw each day. I would like to see
these white ones once again—
as white as clouds, she said, or red as cavan roots
left uncovered in the sun too long.
In photographs of black and white and gray,
what little I can see of the faces of the ladies of the air
seems light as sand or as no color, like the rain.
Medala said there was already

a small peaceful group of people
living on the island
when the shipwrecked ones came here.
The land was lush with fragrant flowers
and all manner of most useful and delicious plants
for which the survivors had no names.
It seemed a paradise,
and some believed that they had died.
A lake was found inland,
so fresh the water glistened in the sun.
Soon distinctions between slave and seller,
native and nonnative, dark and light,
began to cease being made
in efforts that were needed to survive.
Over the years, the former customs of the many tribes
were brought together and the useful ones
accepted by the group
and adopted by the people living here before.
The fact that women should serve men
had been the way for most of the newcomers
but was as foreign to the island people
as the fattening and ceremonial cutting of young women,
and they rebelled against all three.
Yet the original inhabitants were few in number
and the larger group decided
to adopt the ways they had known
so that each woman would be purified
and all wives would stay faithful and content,
while husbands could be guaranteed

a virginal, voluptuous bride.
In spite of death sometimes from the rough surgery,
some painful lifelong consequences,
and much harder births,
the present tribe persists in this unwholesome
practice whose effects can last forever
and diminish a young woman all her life.
I do not like this ending to Aunt Margaret's story.
Her explanations do not tell enough.
Could it be possible that Cousin Ene died this way
while still almost a child?
The thought is hideous,
more so because it seems
as if it might, in fact, be true.
I notice that my aunt
has copied other sentences
along the bottom of the page.
The first is one short line of poetry
with the name *Whitman* after it:
The man's body is sacred
and the woman's body is sacred.
On the next line she has written only "psalm":
I give you thanks, O Lord,
for I am wonderfully made.

The cutting.
I shut the book
and look long into the fire,
knowing there will be no answer there.

I have heard the word before,
but when I asked our mother,
she would not explain, saying only:
"It is not something to be talked about,"
or, *"You must wait until your time.*
Be thankful you are not as young as some."
I had thought perhaps it was like moonflow,
which prepares a place in which a child may grow.
The bleeding stops for months, they say,
each time a seed is planted by a man.
But of what use can this strange cutting custom be?
How is it done? I did not know it can result in death.
What does it mean to say that it *"diminishes a woman"*?
I think that I must ask Miduna once again.
I fear the pain may be much greater
than that which comes each time
my stomach fills with blood and sheds it.
My head is churning with these new facts and feels heavy,
but I do not dare to fall asleep
with this book still in my hand.
I hide it carefully before I close my eyes.

Miduna is attending to her baby at first light.
He has had his fill already
and the corners of his little mouth turn up.
Before she can begin her other rituals,
I ask about the cutting. She turns to me,
her eyes both guarded and surprised.
"Has no one told you yet?"

"It is not because I have not asked.
Mother says the answer
will be given me when I am ready.
Is it something that will happen in my sleep?"
"I wish it could be so," says Miduna.
This answer worries me.
The sharpness of the word itself
is troublesome enough.
"Then," I ask reluctantly, "am I to think
that it is something done to me,
like the scarring of a boy's face
when he becomes a man?"
"It is."
"With a sharp implement?"
"Something swift and sharp."
"And afterward?"
"There will be pain for a while
in the place of the incision."
She glances down to where
the babies leave the mother,
but I have guessed the place.
"Who will do this?"
"Nanina is the one, Toba's assistant."
The thought of Toba descending once again,
this time with old Nanina,
and for such a purpose,
is most horrifying.
I am breathless when I ask,
"Why cannot Aunt Margaret be the one?

She would be gentle and has much healing skill as well."
"She says the custom mutilates, and would refuse.
Also, Nanina is the one skilled in this ceremony,
though other women will be asked to help."
I think about the *Island Story*
and that the hiding of it in a book must be a warning
that I cannot tell Miduna.
But I am desperate to know
when this procedure will be done to me.
"It is best you do not know the time or day,"
says Miduna, as if in answer to my silent thought.
"The worst is over quickly.
There is a drink made from oaxa
that will make the memory of it fade."
She says this last so cheerfully,
as if she speaks of some fine celebration.
"Did it happen so to you?"
Miduna does not answer,
yet I see tears fall down
upon the face of George.
"It is something
of which I cannot speak," she says at last.
"But you must speak to me. I have to know.
Please, Miduna. Tell me what it is Nanina does."
Miduna's breath is faint as dropping leaves.
"You have to promise that you will not tell
another person what I say."
"I swear upon Ossada I will not."
"If you were not my sister..."

But she does not go on
until I question her again.
"Will I be changed in any way?"
She nods, then adds, "In ways
that as a married woman it is best."
She sounds as if she repeats words
exactly as they once were told to her.
"Also, a smaller entrance
to your body will be made,
which will make functions
such as moonflow
somewhat difficult, but you
will grow accustomed in a while."
I do not understand.
"What reason could there be for this?"
Miduna grows annoyed.
"I do not have the answers
for each little thing.
The wise ones of the tribe
made these decisions long before
our mother's mothers woke to life.
Nanina has performed this task for years
and is most thorough."
She coughs a little,
as if what she says now
is of no importance.
"And, of course, with every birth
there is more mending to be done.
Aunt Margaret is allowed to help with this."

Mending? Allowed?
Then suddenly Miduna laughs.
"You, too, will be all stitched shut
like a chicken. Think of that!"
I can imagine it too easily.
Why must my healthy body—anyone's—
be rearranged?
The man's body is sacred
and the woman's body is sacred.
How can it be a good thing
to be changed in ways
the gods did not decree
when I was born?
Aunt Margaret had also written:
"*...whose effects can last forever...*"
I have to ask:
"Is this how Cousin Ene died?"
Miduna stares at me
while holding George against her like a shield.
"That was so long ago!"
"Tell, me, Miduna.
Did Ene die within her father's fattening hut?"
My sister's voice is small and faraway.
"I cannot tell you that."
My own voice shouts so loudly in my heart
I am afraid it can be heard:
It will not happen so to me!

8

Aunt Margaret comes again at dawn.

Again she carries something,

but she does not pass it on to me.

Perhaps she hesitates because Miduna is awake.

"You come so early," Miduna says to Margaret,

her voice still filled with sleep.

"As it is best I should," says Margaret,

and Miduna does not disagree.

We both know that our aunt

would not be welcomed

later by the other women.

At least they could not show

such welcome on their faces.

Outcast is what Father calls her,

and it is the way the men

have treated her for years.

There is much beauty

in her face and body,

inside of her as well,

so this treatment of her

has been a mystery to me.

Could her ability to read be so unsettling,

or is it that she has no children of her own?

"It is for men to know things that are written down,"

our mother told me once

when I complained of such unfairness.
"A woman's brain is best for other things."
"Then why protect it with a head cloth?
Why pretend it has great value?"
These were the reasons given me
when I was very young
for why a woman
wraps her head in colors that are bright.
Even then it made no sense
to revere something
needed only when one plans
to gather wood or count the hens.
"Margaret has her own ways," Mother said,
and there was scorn within her voice,
"that are not of the tribe."
With Aunt Margaret, Miduna is not
gracious as she should be to an elder.
She does not rise or offer
something cool to drink.
This I am quick to do, however,
so I will not suffer shame for both of us.
Aunt Margaret was a favorite of Miduna's
not so many years ago. She was the one
who always helped us with our hair
or wove the cloth for our most colorful danabos.
She listened to us, too, her wide pale eyes
intent on everything we had to say,
while Mother often didn't have the time.
But now my older sister has so changed

in her regard of Margaret,
it is as if she's learned of something
that she did not know before.
I think her thoughts may have been poisoned,
as with the sap of manchineel
upon an arrow's point, and it makes me sad
to see Miduna pull away from her
while I extend both arms for an embrace.
My aunt looks carefully upon me,
not revealing what her new perceptions
of my body's size might be.
There is a flickering concern,
however, guarded deep within her eyes.
Not until Miduna turns to George
does Margaret slip the parcel underneath my mat.
She quickly starts to speak of things
like the weather or the latest baby to be born.
I have always thought it most peculiar
that the same woman who cries out
for Margaret in her childbirth pain
does not acknowledge her upon a village path.
She smoothes the hair back
from my face most tenderly.
"You do look thin," she says at last.
"Too fat may not be good,
  but thin like this and you will soon be sick."
"I do not wish for it," I tell her. "But nothing
  seems to taste the way it should."
"She tries to eat," Miduna says in my defense.

"I think there is a worry god
inside her soul that never sleeps,
or else a large and hungry worm
which steals the morsels for himself."
Aunt Margaret takes the baby in her lap and laughs.
"And is it he who spits the food into the basket?"
I do not think it humorous
that there could be a thing inside of me,
gods or giant worms or anything,
that could control me so.
I do know this: whatever lives so deep
is something of myself,
something of me that cannot yet be seen,
a thing much stronger
than the self I can command.
"I passed Ashani on my way here," Margaret says
while stretching George's tiny arms and legs.
"He was asleep upon the beach."
"He likes it better there
than with his family on some nights."
"Perhaps their peace returns
when he decides to leave," says Margaret.
"Most monkeys are less agitated."
So Ashani has been sleeping on the beach.
Have we walked past him on our way to bathe?
It is so good to know he has been close,
sad to remember that I cannot
hunt or run with him again.
Even when very young,

he seemed to have the energy of two.
Instructed to tend goats,
he'd somehow manage
to make something magical
out of discarded twigs,
invent new games that we could play,
or tell a story that would cause the other children
to assemble at his feet.
When I take time to think of it,
it was our appetite to see,
to know, to do so many things,
that drew us both together from the first.
I know the pictures in the cave
of which Aunt Margaret tells.
I have looked long at how
the women hold their spears
in much the way the men hold theirs.
These women are not over fat;
their heads are not wrapped up in cloth.
"I spoke to him," says Margaret.
"He said that he was glad I had disturbed his sleep.
He had a message for you, Helen."
Miduna looks annoyed and mocks him.
"'Come out, Helen. Let us steal Mototo's leaky boat
and play our silly pranks on sightless Nama.'"
"We never did tease Nama," I protest.
I cannot claim we never stole the boat.
But not once did Mototo miss it. The boat
had made it possible for us

to climb the egg rocks from below
and watch the hatching of the frigates
and the tropicbirds.
And if we anchored far enough away,
we'd spy upon the scientists that come each year
to study these and other nests.
"He wonders when your fattening will be completed,"
says Aunt Margaret. "He needs to hear from you
that you will be the wife of Esenu, as people say.
He thinks it is a joke, a trick, that it cannot be true."
To me it is not true as well.
"At present, Helen may not speak
with men or even boys," Miduna says.
"You know it well, Aunt Margaret.
Ashani must believe what he's been told."
Aunt Margaret takes my hands and holds them.
As she looks down at me,
I know she sees into the part
that even now is trying to break free.
She smiles.
"I can deliver messages. There is no limit
to the things I can remember."
A message. Yes.
But Miduna quickly says,
"I do not think that is allowed as well."
"If it is not allowed, it will be I
who break the law, not Helen."
"And you who pay for it."
Margaret laughs her weary laugh

with edges that are sharp.
"What consequences
are there left for me to pay?"
She turns again to me. "Quickly.
Before the women come.
Tell me the things I need to tell Ashani."
If only Miduna were not listening.
Nothing I can tell Aunt Margaret would surprise her.
But Miduna will repeat all that I say.
I know it and must phrase my message carefully.
"Tell him," I say, my eyes fixed on Miduna,
"that yes, my elders plan that I shall marry Esenu.
They also plan that I shall grow quite fat
before it can be done."
Ashani is sure to understand exactly what I mean.
He knows my willful nature
and will probably not be surprised
at how my stubborn body has behaved.
"Tell him," I say when Margaret
starts to part the reeds within the doorway,
"I look into the trees at twilight."
"What foolishness is that?" asks Miduna.
"You sound as simple as Orena."
"And ask him if," I add, "he has lately been
to see the giant bird with great stiff wings."

9

All day the women come
with food enough to feed
the children of one family.
I have learned to taste each offering,
exclaim upon its excellence, and say
that I will finish it when they have left.
Miduna is the only one not fooled by this.
Keeping up such pretense is exhausting,
and I sleep for hours in between these visits.
When the ones arrive to take the serving bowls away,
I open up my eyes to find Miduna
has consumed her food and mine as well.
Our mother has not been here for some days.
They say she needs to oversee the harvesting of rice,
but I believe she hopes to see improvement in my size
if she puts time between her visits.
She sends our younger sister, Suba,
who is delighted to be here inside the fattening hut,
if only for a while. She is so plump already
that it will not take much to round her out.
Her eyes are bright above the platter that she carries,
but when she sees my face they dim with worry.
"Your cheeks were fatter, Helen, the day you left."
"You know I do not fatten easily."
"Before it was because you ran and jumped so much.

But here there is no place to run"—
she leaps about from one wall to the next—
"and very little space to jump.
What do you do all day?"
She twirls in circles, chattering,
"Instead of you, I now prepare the flax,
help with the weaving,
and to sew the clothes. It's tiresome.
How wonderful to be
so free of duties once again!"
She looks around the room approvingly.
Miduna concentrates upon another basket.
George is fast asleep.
The smell of sweet oaxa covers up most other odors.
"I would gladly trade you places," I tell her.
I notice she is growing taller.
In fact, she seems so changed
in these few weeks that I must ask,
"You have not reached moonflow already, Suba?"
She looks upon her feet as if ashamed.
"Not yet. I wait and wait for it. It will not come."
But then she brightens.
"Mother says that sometimes it is best
to start the fattening in spite of that."
"Why be so eager to grow up?"
I hear Aunt Margaret's voice in mine
when I tell Suba,
"There is a time for everything."
But she begins to pout.

"It is not fair. Why were you born before me?"
She does not understand why I am here.
Like other girls,
she knows so little of our customs
that she would not think to question
those that claim
to change a girl into a woman.
If not for Margaret, perhaps
I would not question things as I do now,
or feel this great need
to protect my younger sister.
It is an unfamiliar feeling toward someone
just one year younger than myself.
Why does Miduna not have
such a wish to protect me?
"Your time will come, Suba," Miduna tells her.
"You will have a baby just like George one day."
Is that what I should want? Is that what Suba wants,
while she is still so much a child herself?
The insects that she catches and collects.
The butterflies she mounts on weathered wood.
What husband, young or old,
will give her time to do such things
or read the books we've shared?
What other dreams does Suba carry in her head?
I need to know but cannot ask her now,
for like the other ones who come and go,
she must not stay. Before she leaves,

she begs me to get fatter soon.
"So we can play our games again."
No. She does not understand this place,
the things that are to come, at all.

I do not take the parcel from beneath my mat
until Miduna is concerned with bathing George
and wrapping him again. Inside
are three small packets, tied with straw.
Letters are inscribed on each.
One packet is for FEAR; another is for PAIN.
The third has smaller letters
that on close inspection read
TO STOP THE BLEEDING.
Within each packet are ground herbs
with smells that are quite strong but unfamiliar.
I picture Margaret grinding them herself
and know that I can trust their use
and the strict dosage she has lettered.
But the fact that she has brought them here today
makes me afraid that I will need them very soon,
much sooner than I thought,
that in this way she has
abandoned me to what will come.
A trembling rises from my center
outward to my fingers and my feet,
making my entire body weak.
A sudden sob escapes my mouth

so loudly that Miduna turns and looks at me.
"What is it now?"
I sit upon the parcel so she will not see it.
I yawn as loudly as I can, so she will think
that such a sound was what she heard.
But I am faint with fear.
The contents of this package
tell me that the cutting time is nearer than I thought.
Aunt Margaret may as well have said in words
that it is up to me how I'll conduct myself,
that she has given all the help she can.
With this peculiar gift
she has now put my care and destiny
into my hands, which are so unprepared.

The day goes on as though within a dream.
All thought has been chased from my mind,
my movements stilled
like those of the tall palm fronds by the door.
The shadows on the walls are growing longer
when I suddenly remember
that it is another twilight in this place.
I look straight up to where the smoke escapes.
There is a patch of deepening blue.
It is so much like looking up into a lake
that I wish with all my strength
for it to spill its banks
and flood me with it from this hut.

I keep my eyes upon the empty blueness.
When they begin to close,
I almost miss the flicker of a hand
the way it quavers up and down
within the opening
just like a solitary wing.

10

All day I force myself to move about,
not wanting to be prone upon my mat
when Toba makes his next appearance.
This dread has driven appetite away completely.
I sip the milk of coconut to calm myself
while Miduna seems to wonder
what additional dark magic has descended.
"You either sleep away the day
   or pace about exactly like a beast."
To please her, I sit cross-legged the way she does
and try to start a basket.
I am so new at this
   my efforts are as clumsy as I feel.
"Thank Ossada you have begun
   to do something of use. Whatever
you imagine, Helen, you will need
some sturdy baskets in your home.
I could pretend that some of mine belong to you,
but anyone would see the difference.
It takes much practice to build baskets
that are both strong and beautiful."
I know that she is right
and that she truly would make
twice as many baskets
if she thought I could not make my own.

From our early years Miduna
has been like a second mother
to both Suba and myself.
It seems so natural
for her to have a family of her own at last.
She guides the reeds within my hands
until I have a reasonable start
and can proceed alone. In time
the steady rhythm of the weaving in and out
begins to comfort me, and for long minutes
I am able to be unaware of all the dread I feel.
In such ways does the morning pass.
Mother does not come to take assessment of me.
The women comment only with their eyes.
The afternoon is damp and hot,
and though I start to pace again,
eventually I stretch upon my mat and sleep.
The dreams are colorful,
and I can fly above the tops of trees.
Up so high, I see beyond the silver line
and wake up with a need
to tell Miduna what I've found there.
But as I try to speak of it,
the dream dissolves into a memory
too indistinct to be described.
I stammer like some little child who talks in sleep.
I have slept away the twilight.
When I look up to the sky,
it is darker than the shadows and no longer blue.

One bright star is visible above a moon
which has a tiny slice removed.
Will it be soon? Tonight?
I tell Ossada
if she spares me through this night,
I will not leave my fate to chance.
In spite of marriage plans for me,
I am a young girl still,
too young, perhaps, to slip away alone
and hide myself. But what else can I do?
Just as the fire starts to die,
the women come again and tend it.
One begins to tell a story of the way
in which the tribe had tricked the English
into leaving them alone some years ago,
and how our tribesmen were so clever
that they took the interlopers' words from them
but gave back nothing in return.
Others have so many things to add
or other tales to tell
that they decide to stay
and form a circle full of story.
Usually I love such times,
but on this night when my mind slips
into the forest paths that they create,
I see myself abandoned there.
Some stories are of spells cast
upon men and women,
of strange creatures, *gimpas,*

that appear at dusk
to take small children to their caves
and change them into creatures like themselves.
I have heard these stories many times before,
but they still have such power over me
that after all the women leave,
I hear each falling coconut outside the door
as if it is a leopard's step or something worse.
I do not sleep. I shiver so Miduna wraps me
almost as she would her child.
She stokes the fire, though the air is hot.
"You see," she says at last.
"Aunt Margaret was correct.
If you refuse to eat,
it is a certainty you will be sick."
She puts her hand upon my forehead
and seems puzzled when she finds it cool.
"Sleep, little cayawolf.
You will feel better when you wake."
Her tender treatment of me is so calming
that I try to do just as she says.
And yet I want to sleep
but wake into the world I knew.
I must remind myself
that something terrible
may soon be visited upon me,
perhaps on this same night.
I must repeat the frightful sharpness
of the *cutting* word within my mind

and tell myself that it is real,
that I cannot relax my guard.

The baby cries. Miduna shushes him—
more, I think, for my sake than for his.
His little noises as he takes the breast
are so trusting and content
they make it difficult for me
to feel the threat I know is there.
Perhaps this night is not the one.
But if not now, then when? What night?
I cannot take the chance
of waiting to find out.
When George falls fast asleep,
Miduna curls protectively around his little form
and sleeps herself. I keep my eyes
upon the reeds within the doorway.
Just the slightest movement of them
makes me cower
and then tremble uncontrollably
until I wonder if it is in fact a fever that I harbor.
How awful to be all alone and sick
within the vast and endless tangle of our island!
Why did I let Ashani
lead me through it all these years?
Why did I not try harder
to remember all its twists and turns myself?
As I attempt to build a picture in my mind
of certain places on the island I can go if I should run,

my thoughts become so trapped inside my fear,
it is a maze I make instead.
Attempts to soothe myself
produce the opposite effect
and make me think my trembling
will be both sensed and heard.
The air itself is colored by the dread I feel.
Grey shadows now are streaked with leaping shapes
of lavender and black.
The way I startle
at the faintest noises just outside,
the way the smallest sound
alarms me so I want to scream—
I have waited long enough.
There is not one thing
left for me to do but act.
On tiptoe I collect the things I plan to take.
But something, just my movements
through the hut perhaps,
awakens George before his feeding time.
Miduna rises with a mother's quick concern.
She picks him up, then looks around at me.
"I thought you would be fast asleep."
"I was. But I felt sick."
"Oh. Not again!"
"I am better now," I say and go back to my mat.
She's clearly unconvinced.
She props herself against a wall
to nurse the baby.

When he is finished, she remains awake.
"You can go back to sleep," I say.
But she insists,
"I will keep you company. I really do not mind."
I yawn as if my own lost sleep
is sneaking up on me.
I close my eyes.
In minutes, when I open them,
she is just staring up into the dark
outside the hut. Her eyes catch mine
before I close them once again.
"Is something wrong?" she asks.
"Hmm?" I answer, as if overcome with sleep.
She rises to place George upon his bed,
but then returns and sits against the wall.
I know that she is watching me.
For hours she remains this way,
and I remain awake behind closed eyes,
imagining the horrors soon in store.
The minutes drip so slowly,
one painstakingly into the next,
I cannot piece the time together
into larger spaces. I do not dare
to thrash around with restlessness
the way that I would like. My muscles ache
as if held in restraint.
Two or three times
I look through closely guarded lids
to see if she is sleeping yet.

Two or three times
her eyes reflect the tiny fire
that we keep throughout the night.
It must be long past midnight
when her little breathy snores
become at last
the signal I have waited for.

I have reached
a little hillock in the dark
by following the paths that lead away
from all the huts within the trees.
From here the sleeping village
stretches out below
like many nests of birds.
As I pause for breath,
my heart within my ears,
the village seems so peaceful
as to make my running seem a crazy thing,
a child's imagining
or the playing of a game.
I check what I have taken with me:
one dull knife,
some wassa cake and roasted nuts,
a pineapple and chunks of coconut,
my book about the ladies of the air,
Aunt Margaret's story of the island,
and the packet of the herbs for fear.
The night is warm,
so I wear a clean danabo only.
My feet have always traveled
over sand and dirt and rocky places.

~~~~~~~~

Looking back, the fattening hut
stands out from all the others,
for it is one of the few upon the ground
and without windows.
A whiff of smoke that trails into the sky
marks it as well. The huts within the trees
are open on three sides, with woven coverings
that can be lowered in the rain and wind.
As watchful as Miduna tried to be,
she is asleep now with her child
and unaware that I have left.
I watch the steady fire of the torches
at the doorway of the hut
that burn throughout the night
as though to guard a shrine.
They cast their flickering light
far into the great shadows all about.
When I climb a tamarind tree
to get a better look, my breathing
leaves my chest in quick and shallow bursts,
my hands and feet both tingle
as they move along the bark.
Exhausted, I rest straddled
on the lowest branch of all.
It is just high enough for me to see
the darkened village and a great expanse of sea,
the moonlit water rolling in and out
so silently, as if all life
could be so undisturbed.

Suddenly I see a path of light,
fire patterns bobbing up and down
in strange and wavy lines. I think
the fire must be carried, for it travels
in a measured way from the outer edges
of the village to the lighted space
before the doorway of the hut.
Once it arrives inside
that circle made of light,
I see that there are many torches
in the hands of men.
In front of them a feathered figure
prances up and down, his chants
rise up into the trees.
The others answer him
until the song is chilling and intense.
A woman dressed in scarlet
weaves her fingers through the air
as she begins to sway and join the chant.
The feathered figure. It can only be the Healer, Toba!
It is Nanina who is swaying back and forth
with several other grandmothers,
all brightly dressed,
who must have come to help.
Aunt Margaret was right,
and I have put the signs together well.
This *is* the night of which she told me
And the thought

that I have just escaped in time
is like a sudden blow
that makes me motionless with fear.
I watch, transfixed
by what is going on so far below me
and by what would certainly
have happened there
if I had stayed.
The shrill call of the killy killy
seems to be a warning signal telling me
that just as soon as those men
find me gone, they'll go in search of me.
They are much swifter, stronger,
and more cunning than I am,
and so I cannot spend more time here
watching what is going on below,
even if they do not
go inside the hut until the dawn.
More breathless than before,
I slip down from the tree,
gather my supplies,
and start to run, to stumble,
through the forest growth, outside the paths,
as if I know the way. Where is Ashani
when I need him here to lead me?
How will I manage to survive?
I have some sense
of which direction I should take
and of the many obstacles

I might encounter on the way.
There are salt ponds around the island
that I must avoid, and though I am still far
from the large pond that many call a lake,
the odor of still water is a thing
familiar to me. I have read
how this same skill is owned
by the great animals called elephants,
which we have never seen upon our island.
Speed and vigilance
will help me to avoid the poisonous lizards,
and I must also move as quickly as I can
in order not to feel
the rough vines and sharp rocks.
Until I stop again for breath
I am quite unaware
of all the burning in my ankles and my feet.
When with Ashani
we could see what was before us
in the light of day. I must not
slow my steps and cannot see ahead
except where moonlight lays a trail.
Where trees are few the way is clear;
where there are many
I am better hidden but must go more slowly.
The search drums have begun
to pound into the night.
They are rarely used,
and almost always

when a man is lost at sea.
I picture women spilling
from their hammocks
and descending from the trees
to see the reason for the drums.
I picture Mother
wailing when she learns
that it is Helen whom they seek.
I feel her deep disgrace.
The tears that come to me hold all
my shame and sorrow
and my defiance and great fear as well.
How can I bear the mixture of such things?
And yet I must. Miduna
is not here to intercede for me. Perhaps
she would not want to, knowing now
that I have tricked her.
At first she will believe
it is a child's game, that I cannot
be so far away and will return by morning.
As soon as possible, however, I must
find a hiding place so safe and secret
that no one with torches or sharp knives
can find me. It must also be a place
Ashani might expect that I will go to.
I have a skin of water in my pack
yet do not take a drink
until my throat is parched
and my dry tongue begins

to swell within my mouth.
It seems that I have run for hours,
yet the depth of dark surrounding me
leads me to know
that it is hours still before first light.
I feel that I could drop right down
in any spot I find myself,
but then the water buoys me
just enough to keep
one foot before the other.
Though the unfamiliar pangs
of hunger make my progress harder,
I cannot afford the time
that it would take to stop and eat.
Thoughts of the soft voice of Miduna
and of Mother's great warm lap
make me quite desolate.
Only Aunt Margaret
would be willing
to give comfort to me on this day,
and she is much too far from me.
Hers is the first hut
they will search for me as well,
since, like her, I have defied
the tribal customs
and refused a sacred ceremony.
Slowly my eyes become
accustomed to the dark
and I can pick out objects at a distance.

A gecko hangs down from a branch
and glistens until I spot it—
just before it falls upon my neck.
A family of long-snouted anteaters
retreats into the forest while young
cayawolves cry out
against the rumble of the drums.
At times I think I hear the thunder
of the searchers' feet,
or feel it through my own,
but I dare not look around;
at times the air is still enough
for me to hear the drumming of my heart.
Whenever I must stop for breath,
there is a patter like an echo of my steps.
It is always so, and I begin to think
that it is *gimpas* on my trail.
But it is long past dusk, the time
when they are said to have been seen.
Are they invisible in darkness?
And if so, would it be possible
for them to capture me,
as in the stories I've been told?
There are no caves in this direction,
the places where they are believed to live.
It would take many little *gimpas*
just to drag a girl as tall as I am
all across the island, even though
I am so weakened and worn down.

In fact, the sound I hear is much too faint
to be caused by a host of little creatures.
Perhaps it is a leopard stalking me,
or a lone tribesman who has run ahead
of all the rest. I stop.
There is the patter.
I run and stop again.
The patter follows.
I cannot outrun it.
I cannot see it.
I must pretend to be alone and safe.
I must continue to pretend
and must not rest.

A bright yellow bananaquit
lands close to me.
It is the first thing I see
after opening my eyes.
Then I find a thicket
of dead vines above my head,
and many thrashers
pecking at the berries
where the vine is living still.
When I try to stretch,
my arms and face are scratched
by all the tiny matted twigs that enclose me.
At first I see no opening
within my cage, and I think
the *gimpas* must have captured me.
Then I remember thrusting my whole self
into this thicket in the darkest part of night,
before the dawn, when
I could go no further.
My bruised feet, in fact,
are sticking out,
and I soon find that if I shimmy
on my stomach I can back out slowly
from this most unpleasant place.
Once free, my head whirls

every time I try to stand,
and I must seek
the safety of the ground again.
The hunger of last night has left me,
but before I can go on, I'll have to eat.
Devouring wassa cake for breakfast
is agreeable.
I cut a piece of pineapple
and let the juice
run freely down my hands and arms.
My danabo is now sticky, too, and muddy.
The air is thick with birdsong; nothing more.
I hear no movement in the brush,
no voices of a band in search of me.
Perhaps the search did not begin—
perhaps they think I will return
after some hard days spent
in wandering the island all alone,
and do as I am told.
Perhaps old Esenu
has told the tribe to wait.
It would indeed be like a gift,
but one I cannot count on,
since it must be easier
to groom an island bride
than go in search of one
across the silver line
in places he has never been!
At least the quiet pattering has ceased.

If it had been an animal, I would not now
be sitting on this rock but up a tree, or eaten.
It is so cool and silent at this hour,
I feel a wish to stay just where I am
and sleep away the day.
But it would lose me precious time.
In daylight I can see the thicket that I chose
is not a hiding place at all.
Anyone who comes this way
could see me here and make use of it
as a convenient trap. Already insects
are attracted to my sticky hands and face,
yet there is not an ocean here to wash in.
I lick my lips before I realize
my tongue will come back
coated with small bitter bugs
and I must spit them all away.
I take a swallow from my water skin
and feel whatever little bugs are left
slide down my throat. There are
so many singing birds here it is hard
to be disgusted or afraid. It sounds
just like a day when we
would run off for adventure,
just Ashani, sometimes Suba, and myself.
That I will never have those days again
is quite the hardest thing to understand.
The air is heavy with the smell of salt,
and as I come across the rise

I see one of the island ponds,
small sections rimmed in low walls of stone,
wide twisting strips of water that are pink
while overlapped in green.
There are some piles of salt
along the shore,
and men and women both
have waded out to pole
a wide flat-bottomed boat
in which they place thick cakes of salt.
Some workers carry boxes of it on their heads
and empty it in barrels. When the barrels fill,
the men will take them overland
right to the ocean's edge
and onto little boats again
and then to one large ship that waits
where water holds the sky.
I've seen the last part many times.
I cannot leave the safety
of the trees to go around the pond
or they will surely see me. Before they do,
I climb a tamarind tree and settle in the crook of it.
At first it is most comfortable and cool,
but soon the rough hard bark
against my back and bottom
makes me squirm. My hunger pangs
are now as strong as in my life before,
when each day was so simple
and just waiting with discoveries.

I welcome these familiar pangs,
these feelings from that earlier time, until
my thirst and hunger are intense enough
to cause a dull and throbbing pain.
Since I have foolishly
left my food and water on the ground below,
all I can do is clutch myself
and cry without a sound.
I cry for pain. I cry for loneliness. I cry for fear.
My knees, pulled up beneath my chin,
become a sopping place on which
to lay my head
before I, mercifully, sleep.

It is the silence that awakens me.
The sun is so much lower in the sky
that everything is dusted in a glow of red.
Two pintail ducks are paddling near the shore.
An egret wades in the same spot
where there were workers earlier.
Right now there isn't anyone around at all.
When I am sure of this,
I climb down to the ground
and grab at tamarind pods,
break them apart,
and suck the sticky seeds.
This does not quench my thirst;
and a banana and the rest
of the baked sweet potato

make it worse.
There are perhaps two swallows
left within my water skin. I take one
and then quickly tie it up. As children
we were told we should not drink
the brackish water in these ponds,
but could it really be so bad?
Walking down the hillside to the water's edge,
I think I hear the patter-pat again,
like rain upon a roof of thatch,
but when my bare feet
hit the sand, the patter stops.
As it gets dark, I must travel
halfway around this water,
keeping to the edges
so as not to lose my way.
The setting sun throws little glints
into the deepest parts until the water seems
quite clear and beckons me. My throat
is rough and hot as sand as I wade out
just like the workers and bend down
until my face is close enough
to feel the water on my lips.
"*No!*"
At this loud outburst
I am so shaken that I nearly topple in.
When I stand up again and turn,
I see a figure, just inside the trees,
who steps out quietly

into the slowly dimming light.
I must squint to make it out.
It is more curiosity I feel than fear,
for though my mind keeps telling me
that I should run, my body won't obey.
And then the figure moves well forward
and removes a cloak the color of the leaves.
"Aunt Margaret!" I cry, rushing toward her arms.
"You did not think that I
would let you run off by yourself,"
she says. She pulls me close to her
and strokes my knotted hair.
I hug her just as hard as I can manage.
"Until I saw you bend to take
a drink of that foul water,
my plan was to keep
well out of your sight."
"I never guessed that you were near,
though you were not
as silent as you thought."
She laughs her lovely, warm, familiar laugh.
"It is these feet," she says, sticking one out.
"A man's feet on the body of a girl. A cruel trick."
Her feet look beautiful to me.
The light touch of her hand upon my cheek
makes fear dissolve until she says,
"Sweet Helen, you are safer by yourself, I think."
She pours fresh water from a large bag
into mine, which is quite small.

"I will not be so far away."
   She starts to back into the trees.
"You cannot leave me here!" I whine,
   exactly like the cayawolf
   Miduna says I mimic.
"I think you know the way.
   I think you know a great deal, Helen,
   and will be just fine. Your instincts
   telling you to travel by the night are good."
   And then she turns and runs and fades,
   just disappears into the forest as I watch.
"Wait!" I cry.
   But she is gone from me
   as swiftly as she came.

I push through frangipani trees
at just the place I saw her fade
so like a magic creature or a dream.
How could she disappear like that
into the forest air?
Why did I let her
take her arms from me
and back away?
I should have cried more, wailed
a little harder. Now
I throw myself upon the sand
and cannot stop the tears
from puddling within my ears
and dripping down my neck.
I feel much more alone
than when I didn't know she followed,
and can hardly raise myself
to travel on. If only
I could wade across the pond,
but Ashani says within my head
that it is deeper than it looks.
The water is no longer pink;
the green is the same color
as the thickest trees.
Any searcher coming here

will have as little trouble spotting me
as he would those yellowlegs
highstepping through the weeds.
When I begin to travel on again
they spread their wings
and rise before my face,
like long-legged bats.
Along the shore there is
hard scratchy stubble
and some very rocky places.
I must move carefully around
the mounds of prickly pear.
A night heron sleeps folded in a tree.
The shine upon the water is
a path, made by the rising moon,
that leads nowhere. Just like
the one I'm making for myself,
I think. My path, too, may soon
dissolve in shadow
or in something worse.
Yet I must go
in the direction
that I seem to know.
There is no other choice.
I miss the patter-pat
that made me feel
as if I was not all alone. How
can Aunt Margaret follow
when she keeps at such a distance

that I neither see nor hear her?
Will she not be discovered
by the very ones in search of me,
and punished for her help?
But then I think
how she is cleverer
than anyone within the tribe.
And yet she is alone,
almost more so than I.
When I call out her name,
the words sail off until
I am a blowpipe shooting them
into black empty space.
There is no answer
and so nothing left for me to do
but keep each stinging foot in motion.
Halfway around the pond
I notice something glowing
at the place where
I must enter trees again.
It is not bright enough
to be a fire, more like a poinciana tree
aglow at sunset. It does not waver
like a smoldering torch.
The thought occurs
that I should run the other way—
but into what? Better to hope
the glow is coming from some plant
I do not know. The *gimpas*

are said to have no need of light
of any kind. There is no
moving shadow and no sense
of any living thing in wait for me.
Approaching, I see the glow
comes from the ground.
Perhaps it is a phosphorescence
like the surface of the bay
when it is filled with
tiny shining creatures.
Closer still, it becomes clear
that I am seeing embers of somebody's
recent fire. The evening is not cold
enough for me to need the heat,
but I stand near it
in order to be touched
by something warm.
Who was just here?
When did they leave?
Could they have caught
a glimpse of me
or of Aunt Margaret
from across the pond?
Was it a group
of tribesmen, or just one?
Where did he, where did they, go?
Which way? I cannot see
clear footprints in the sand

in this weak moonlight.
My own prints fade away from me
as I approach a cordia tree,
in search of small round fruit
in darkness. Most that I find
are bruised or rotting,
but I am famished
for the moisture of their flesh
and feel exhausted,
just as if I hadn't slept the day
within the safety of a tree.
There is a blue snake
hanging from a branch,
a type that I have never seen,
yet I have known since childhood
that there are no poisonous ones
upon the island. Maybe the dark
makes it appear so very blue.
In case it is a messenger
or sign, I try not to disturb it
as it twists down to the ground
and disappears as quickly
as my aunt. If anyone could turn
herself into a snake or any other animal
it would be her. What better way
to watch me? Perhaps
this is her secret,
for it often seems to me

that she possesses powers that are magical.
I believe the others
have this sense of her as well
and that is why they fear her so.
And yet she's never boasted
of such things. It is enough
that I feel certain she will reappear
whenever I should need her most.
Certain, and yet in dread
that she will be prevented
in some way.
The tamarind and mango leaves
are turning in a sudden breeze.
The flattened ping of rain upon them
echoes softly one tree to the next.
In only minutes more,
the forest canopy begins to weep
just like a leaking roof of thatch.
The embers sizzle as they die,
and my own hair is streaming.
It is a welcome thing
to have the dust of two days
washed away. I lift my
face, my mouth as open
as a cup. I unwrap my danabo
and raise both my arms
as if to praise Ossada
or whatever god
has granted me this bath.

The blue snake slithers
from its hole and right across
the soggy path
I have begun to trample
for myself.
Then it is gone.

14

There is another small hill up ahead
of which I have no memory.
By night its foliage is
all shades of lavender,
the shadows washed in purple light,
a polished purple crest.
As I come over it, I stumble up against
one of the mounds beneath
large boxes for the dead.
This is a place that I have been
so many times before
to celebrate the journey of a spirit
from this world unto the one unseen.
I have arrived here from another way, however.
In the radiance cast by this pale moon
I see that there are flowers laid
across some of these boxes, like a coat.
Their fragrance makes the stillness
present, as a sound.
For minutes it is
just as if I am no longer
frightened and alone.
A memory slowly comes
of how the women said
the *gimpas* will not enter places

where the dead
may be. Why not, then, rest here
with my ancestors and revered friends?
I curl against the mound nearest
the place where a small piece of ocean
can be seen if it were day.
The breeze is warm, the silence
full of kindness and regard.
It is the safest I have felt
for many days. I lean against
the grassy slope and sleep.

The noise of many flutes and tambourines
awakens me, and from the corner of my eye
I watch a small procession wind its way
between the mounds to one that lies
some distance from the place
which I have chosen as a bed.
The women wail most properly
and tramp the incline with their bodies bent
in deep despair. One mourner rests her arms
upon a woman on each side of her
and keens. To my astonishment,
it is Aleda's face I see when
this, the saddest of all persons, lifts her eyes.
Her younger brothers and some other members
of the tribe carry the burial box,
which, I guess from observing
how Aleda is so grieved,

must hold the Healer, Toba.
Though it is known
that the great burden of so many years
cannot be cured,
I wonder why,
with all the powers that he claimed,
he could not heal himself.
The people carry bougainvillea tendrils,
armfuls of gardenia blossoms,
giant yellow, pink, and red hibiscus blooms.
They pile these on the box
until no wood at all is seen.
On top of this Aleda
lays the feathered cloak, the mask and headdress,
with great care. This single gesture
quiets any doubt at who is being buried here.
I wince at just how limp and powerless
the costume of importance looks
upon the flower pile.
Nanina starts to chant the prayers
to Hamani, the ones the living
offer up at every death
to beg a welcome for this spirit
and a place of peace for it to rest.
I watch my father and my brothers
mouth the words, as I have seen
them do so many times before.
No women from our family are present.

No doubt our mother and my sister Suba, too,
are absent out of shame for me.
Miduna would not be allowed
to leave the hut, of course,
because she nurses still.
Before Nanina can say many words
of the first incantation, Habad
storms up from the gathering crowd,
a tuberous young male
with wide-spaced ears,
and motions her away.
Confused, she staggers
to the edge of the large group.
I quickly move
to where I won't be seen
but find that it is harder now
for me to view the service for myself.
Habad takes over
where Nanina stopped.
He is the only son of Toba's oldest wife
and will succeed his father
as the healer of our tribe.
No one questions his sole right
to lead the prayers—
or his swift show of rudeness
to an elder woman of the tribe.
Afterward, there is a moaning
from the group which weaves

in deep, despondent tones
all through the burial mounds.
When it begins to fade
with the descent of all the mourners
on their way back to our village,
I take a small chance
that I might be seen
and watch the last ones leave.
Aleda still remains beside the grave,
alone like a lost little girl.
No longer does she keen,
but real tears stream over her face.
I strain to hear the words
she alternately shouts
and whispers to the ghost.
"What will I do?
With Habad now in charge,
my own child yet to be
will have no standing.
None at all. Where will we go?"
I long to call her name and say,
"Aleda, come with me."
But I am still not sure
of where it is I go.
At last she throws herself upon the grave
and remains lying there so long
I think she sleeps.
I stay exactly where I am and do not stir.
When dusk arrives she slowly lifts herself

as if she were as large as Mother
and begins to leave.
I wrap my arms about my chest
and squeeze my eyes so tightly closed
that my head starts to throb,
to keep from running after her.

15

As I walk on,
the forest dwindles
on the other side
of this small place of graves.
Before long trees are sparse
and there are spaces of wide sky,
some clouded over,
others spattered with white stars.
Soon there is an opening,
as peaceful as a place
that I have read about
called *meadow.*
In the dark, I cannot see the cactus
that the English called the pope's nose,
which grows almost everywhere.
When I step down on one, my fist flies
hard against my teeth to stifle
a sharp cry. The cactus pricks
most painfully when by surprise.
I must make certain
to pull out every quill
so that the blood runs freely,
the way Ashani once told me.
Here the heavy oleander fragrance
and not the piercing smell of salt,

washes the night.
It is a sleepy odor causing me to yawn
until I wonder if the flower's
poison can be carried on the air,
and if this may not be
the safest place to rest.
I start to run again,
right through high weeds,
in the direction of another stand of trees.
This field is wider than it seemed at first,
the grasses tall enough
to make it difficult to run, each blade a knife.
Their tips are rinsed in yellow
long before I reach the trees, for the sun
is rising like a golden fruit, its juices
staining what is left of dark.
In the honeyed light
I think I see the blue snake,
but my glimpse of it
is too quick to be sure.
There is, however, one surprising stretch
of flowers blue as plumage
on a mass of beautiful rare birds.
They seem to watch me
from their centers
like so many wide clear eyes,
their fragrance as familiar and illusive as
some long-remembered spice or salty breeze,
as they make a path that leads

out from the edges of the meadow
to one tree within a cluster
of wild seaside grapes.
Attached to it is something small and flat
that waves with every gust.
When I come close
I laugh to see a clumsy paper plane,
the silhouette of one
much like the wreck right near the lake.
The nose of it is like an arrow
pointing far off to the right and not directly
through the stand of loblollies in front of me,
which I would otherwise have chosen as the way.
"Ashani," I cry out.
As when I called Aunt Margaret's name,
the word hangs in the air,
not having anywhere to go.
It was a comfort on my tongue,
and I repeat it once again
with little sound.
Now it is day,
I need to hide myself
inside this grove and sleep.
The quiet is so vast it feels
as if there cannot be another person
anywhere for miles.
The searchers must have stopped.
Perhaps it was because of Toba's death.
Perhaps they never started out at all.

Because I cannot know, I climb
another bushy tamarind and try to sleep,
not soundly, for I'm certain if I do I'll surely fall.
A baby monkey swings away and screeches
as I lift myself into his tree. The mother
scoops him up and flies from branch to branch,
scolding loudly as she goes.
I fit myself into a solid crook
where three large branches meet,
but not before I eat a mango
I have picked along the way
and all the nuts that still remain. There
is no food left in my pack. Mother
would be pleased to see my appetite return,
but I begin to wonder if it cannot now be tamed.
I have no memory of how sleep falls over me,
but I awaken just as soon
as voices interrupt my dreams.
They are so close I freeze against the bark
and do not breathe.
From this hiding place I recognize the
mottled head of Esenu.
Miduna's husband, Dar, is with him,
and the two of them
keep looking up into the trees.
I shut my eyes,
hoping, like a hiding child, that if
I do not look into each face,
I cannot then be seen.

This time, I have left nothing at the base.
They walk around within the grove,
startling the young monkeys into
throwing seaside grapes.
As each man tries to dodge the pelts,
he ducks with eyes upon the ground,
and that is how they pass below my tree.
How strange to see them carrying
spears, as if it is wild animals
they seek and not a very frightened girl.
I keep my breathing silent as a thought.
They move some paces down and squat
to rest and take out pipes.
"Foolish girl," I hear Dar telling Esenu.
"Why would she run from someone
  who is able to take care of her so well?"
"It is humiliating
  for a man such as myself."
"For which she must be beaten."
Esenu pulls hard upon his pipe
  and hums agreement.
Dar scratches his big head of wiry curls.
"Miduna is not anything like Helen.
  She is obedient and lives to please me."
"As any woman should."
Dar is such an ordinary, rather stupid man.
Miduna is quite clever. Why
  should she live for him?
Why change her body, be *diminished*,

scar what once was beautiful,
for this or any man?
The psalm Aunt Margaret
copied in her island story—
I give you thanks, O Lord,
for I am wonderfully made—
streams through my mind
in letters that are large.
I want to scream at Esenu and Dar
as loudly as a monkey would,
and need to crush my mouth
against my palm to silence
what is surging to my lips.

It seems they will stay resting here
for hours. Each time they move about,
I crouch in fear. My feet
have gone to sleep, one hand is numb.
At last they rise and tap their pipes
against the very tree in which I sit.
I cannot understand
how they don't sense me here.
But presently, as if each man has heard
an order called from far off,
they tie their spears
upon their backs and sprint away.
Until I can no longer hear
them rustling through the brush,
I do not dare to move.

16

A certain feeling
to the light
tells me
it is already afternoon.
My hunger rises in my gut like thirst
into my mouth, and yet I hesitate
to come down from this spot,
for fear there are
more tribesmen on my trail.
A mother monkey in a nearby tree
grooms her baby with such care
I start to cry again.
It seems that tears are always
waiting in my eyes until
I must waste half the water
that I drink this way. Does
not Aunt Margaret know
my water skin will soon need
filling once again, that I have
no food left within my pack?
When the protective monkey
feeds plump berries to her child,
I have a sudden wish
that I were back inside the hut,
where every kind of food

I could imagine
had been spread before me.
To drive this thought away,
I think of the quick glimpse I had
that made me wonder why
the area beneath Miduna's belly
seemed so different from my own.
The sudden thought occurs
that I have never truly seen
the entire unclothed body
of another woman, even Mother.
Miduna calls it *modesty*, but now I think
it must be *shame*,
for even girls as old as Suba
swim uncovered.
Although I am
of marriageable age, Miduna
did not comment on my nakedness
the nights when we went bathing.
I think how
after the same ceremony
I have just escaped
it would have been
quite different. My body
would have then possessed
those very secrets
every island woman
hides. I also wonder,
with a feeling much like sorrow

or of loss—
since even mother monkeys
care so for the bodies of their children—
why did not Mother, or Miduna even,
care enough for mine?
Or do they truly think the cutting custom
will protect me in some way?
If I am spared by Mother's god, Ossada,
or by this unknown one called *Lord*,
I will not fail my sister Suba
in the way that those I trusted
have failed me.

I sleep again
but wake when it is black
as a cold fire pit.
I have no sense of how much
of the night has passed
until I leave the grove
and step again into the clearing,
where I see the moon
has started falling in the sky.
The paper plane still waves upon the tree.
I tuck it in the waist of my danabo
and set off in the direction that it points.

Long before morning,
the smell of water, fresh
and very near, makes

me start looking for
the inland lake. When it appears,
it is a long and treeless shimmer
and a twin in color to the sky.
A plump crescent moon
is floating in it and makes
everything seem upside down
and me so dizzy that I fall
upon the rocky bank
and must lie flat awhile before I right myself.
I have not eaten for some time,
and yet the wish to splash in this clear water
is much stronger than my need for food.
Its coolness makes me feel less weak;
it is so clean I fill my water skin.
I have caught fish here,
with Ashani, in our bare hands.
Could I be quick enough
to catch the silver ones
that dart about my legs?
Do I remember
how to light a fire? There was
hot sun on all those aimless days.
With none above now, and no flint,
no spark can start,
and so no fish for breakfast.
By morning there are
three small boats upon the water.
Most of the day

I travel well within
the cover of the trees
or climb another bushy one and sleep.
My progress is so slow this way,
it makes me want to weep again.
This time, to stop the tears and a dull anger
that has been welling up—and growing
ever since my first days in the hut—
I take a chance again of being seen
and make one running dive into the chilly lake.
I slip out quickly, then thread my way
back through the forest growth.

Dar and Esenu must not
have seen the paper plane
or known that it was meant for me.
I think they are quite far from here by now,
and yet I startle at each sound.
I have come a distance in this way
when I feel a pounding in the ground beneath my feet
and I scramble up the nearest tree.
There is no place in it where I can truly perch,
but in an instant a large pack
of wild and snorting pigs
rumbles below in such distress
that I believe they must be chased.
After every single squealing one has passed,
I wait for their pursuers.
Just when I think there may be none,

and I am starting down
to pick another hiding place,
three of my tribesmen
race out from the woods,
with arrows and strong bows.
Terrified I have been seen,
I scramble back up to the perch I left
and stay quite still, become
a branch that cannot sway,
until their chatter to each other
and the thumping of their feet
cannot be heard.
Through a veil of leaves I glimpse
another bed of embers on the shore,
that no one tends. It must belong
to some of those who are out in the boats.
I slide down to the ground
and get as near to it
as I am able to
while still within the trees.
Just as I thought, there is some food
left roasting on the coals,
and, like the snake,
I slither on my stomach
through the grass and weeds
until I am beside the fire's edge
and clearly see
the fat plantains and yellow corn.
They give off such a sweet aroma

my saliva starts to gather
at the corners of my mouth.
Quickly I reach out
to take hot pieces of each one
and wrap them up in my danabo.
I stick my singed and smarting fingers
into coarse wet sand before I slither back.
I did not want to steal the food.
I have not stolen anything before
and would not now if there was
any other thing to eat.
Ossada knows that this is true.
I climb a tall mahogany,
become a monkey, eating as I go.
The leaf clusters
protect me well,
but I eat much too quickly.
My insides, eager for each bite,
begin to cramp, and I must force myself
to chew this unexpected meal more slowly.
Sleep is sifting over me like mist,
but I remain on guard
because I roost here like some bird.
Unlike a dove or chinchary,
I have no talons to attach me to a branch.
It is a long fall to the ground,
and I refuse to break my bones.
It is a fight to sleep in little fits this way.

———————

Near dusk I hear
the people in the boat return.
They have strong shoulders
like my brothers and move gracefully
while framed in halos of the setting sun.
Their fire went out long ago,
but the delicious food should still be warm.
Their voices carry
all their upset and surprise
when they discover some is missing.
"It cannot be animals," I hear one say.
"Nothing else has been disturbed."
I fear they will come looking for
the predator within this grove,
but they are more intent on
stoking up the fire for the fish
they carry on a string.
Still, I stay quiet as I can.
Before too long a narrow raft
is poled along the shore,
pulled up, and left.
The man puts his long pole
across it and retreats into the forest,
heading for his home perhaps.
If I had such a raft
I would be saved the journey
all around the lake.
I am not proud that I have had to steal,
I do not want to do it once again,

but will it be a theft, exactly,
if I leave the raft across the water
where its owner will most surely
find it in the light of day?
The men eat their fish supper,
douse the fire, and then gather up
the scraps to take along.
They seem to have forgotten
that a scavenger helped herself
to their small feast. Their voices
in the dusk are softened and resemble
the familiar murmurs of my family
sharing a good meal together.
How I miss
the soft low voices of my brothers
mixed with all the lighter singing sounds
my sisters and our mother make.
After a while
they do not speak,
for they are making
preparations to depart.
When they set off,
it is so very still.
The water laps against the shore in little slaps.
A blue heron with a yellow crown
lands suddenly and pecks at scraps.
He settles like some king
upon the raft and seems to see
right into where I roost within the leaves.

Surely it must be another sign!
I clamber from my perch.
I make quite sure
there's no one else about,
step clumsily aboard the raft,
and pole it slowly out beyond the reeds.

Only a short way into the crossing,
the pole is useless.
I forgot the water would get deeper.
I have no paddle, yet I find
the raft so narrow
I can lie upon my stomach
and use my hands as oars.
Since I lack strength
to paddle in this way for long,
sometimes I'm forced to rest
and let the current or the wind
take charge. It is too dark to find
my bearings by some object
on the shore ahead, and so
I have no way of knowing
if my course is true.
I cannot think
how this new problem can be solved.
First, I must get to land again.
I am soaked through
and shiver in the colder air of night.
The chill has quieted my sore and painful feet
but causes every bone to ache.
Aunt Margaret must have lost my trail by now.
The thing I hope for, what I half expect,

is that Ashani will be waiting
when I pull up to the shore.
But it is such a slow ride
that I fear I will be out here
in the middle of the lake
in broad daylight.
This causes me to gather
all my dwindling strength
and paddle until both my arms
are sore from rubbing up against
such rough bare wood.
The steady movement
chafes my skin until
it is all red and raw.
"Please be there, Ashani,"
I say this many times out loud
to keep the pain from
causing me to stop my paddling.
There are thin stripes of blood
along the wooden edges
that get washed away
each time a hand and arm
dip back into the lake.
Why did the width of all this water
seem so narrow when I started out?
The more I paddle, the more water
flows behind me. By night
I know the shoreline only
by the place the shining stops.

At last the darker shapes
along it are becoming large
enough for me to recognize
a clump of yuccas,
then a slender rim of trees.
But there is nothing
moving as I hoped, no familiar
calling, leaping shape.
A strong persistent breeze
has started blowing at my back.
I stop all motion, hang my arms
straight down into the lake
and rest. The raft glides
on for longer than I know,
and then with one hard jolt
it strands itself
upon a little beach.
I have no strength at all
with which to move,
so I fall fast asleep face down.
I do not know how long I lie this way,
but when the birds of morning,
the rude thrashers and the warblers,
start announcing the new day,
it is clear to me I must move on.
Yet I am frozen to these boards,
my arms too sore and stiff to push me up.
My danabo is still dripping wet
and spotted with dark blood.

The paper plane is soaked and shredded.
The only other things
I carry now, besides my knife,
is my full water skin and two damp books,
and I can hardly bear
the weight of them within my hand.
I wish now that I brought
along the herbs for pain.
I had saved the ones for fear
in case such feelings
should become unbearable,
but I lost them to the lake.
Foggy shapes of boats appear,
and those of fishermen
casting lines through mist.
They are so far away,
to them I must appear like nothing more
than a large piece of wood
beached on the sand.
Because it is too difficult for me to move,
I fall asleep again
and wake up with strong midday sun
upon my back. It was a dangerous thing to do,
my staying out here in the light of day.
At last I find that I can raise my head
and see this is a small protected place
with very little space to land a craft
of any kind. I hear no voices,
yet I cannot trust this luck too long.

I take long drinks of water,
which is now quite warm. It gives me
energy enough to help me up
and slowly back into the lake,
where cooler water soothes
my aching head and arms,
refreshes my parched throat.
I sink my body, tip
my head back, let my hair
float out like grass.
I shut both eyes.
When I open them,
there is a small and very solemn boy
cross-legged on the raft.
He skips flat stones across the water
and does not look at me at all.
It is as though
I am a shorebird stopping here
that he has seen a hundred times before.
I am quite close enough
to notice that his eyes are blue as Margaret's eyes,
an oddity seen rarely on this island.
His skin is much the color of my own.
Even when I stand and wring my hair out
with both hands, he doesn't really look at me.
He seems too young to be a scout
sent on ahead. A spy would
surely run and tell the tribe.
As I emerge through weeds and slimy silt

he suddenly jumps up and comes to meet me,
stretching out his hand
and slipping it in mine
as trustingly as if he's come
to take me home.

18

The pressure of his hand is sweet,
and since I have no notion
if my landing spot is near
or far from where I want to be,
I go with him.
It is the only choice.
Yet when I try to speak,
the words stay in my head.
It is an effort just to walk along
beside this little boy
who has said nothing yet himself,
and has not given me a name
or told me of our destination.
Perhaps he thinks he rescues me.
Perhaps, in fact, he does.
But who will be there
in this place to which he leads?
I know I should be cautious,
yet I feel so like a child myself,
one who cannot think
of what the questions are
that should be asked.
There are few trees along this side
of the lake. The land he leads me over
is quite flat, and studded

with fat bristly shrubs.
I have to stop from time to time
to pull sharp prickers from between my toes
and his. He does not whine
or whimper as most children would.
After a while I need to rest
and find that I can tell him so.
He nods and we both sit upon a large flat stone.
I give him water and take some myself.
I have no food to offer him;
he does not ask for any.
I am too tired to feel hungry.
The sun's hot breath
saps all the strength I still have left.
Sleep. I need to sleep again.
But this most curious child
is tugging on my hand.
"Get up," he says, his voice as small
as he is. "We must hurry."
I want to ask him why, but know
before I even form the question
that I will not understand the answer.
It is so like the times
when I was pulled along by Mother
and no higher than her hip.
I would not think
to question where we went.
He starts to hum.
His thin voice next to me

sounds far away. It is a tune
that I have heard before,
but when?
As sun continues to envelop
this dry sweep of vast unshaded earth
I start to stagger,
yet the boy plods steadily
and still holds tightly to my hand.
I concentrate on patterns
made by rock and earth and cactus
and no longer look
to see where we are headed.
I do not think of time of day,
of time at all, or any other thing
than that we stay in motion
and I have this oddly quiet company.
From time to time
I lose a sense of where we seem to be.
There are long stretches
that are empty of all images and feeling.
No longer do I know if I am tired
but only that I still exist and move ahead.
When a cold shadow falls across my back
it startles like a soft caress, and I look
up into a glade so green
it seems to draw my spirit
into every leaf. The boy
has climbed a mango tree
with the quickness of a cat

and is throwing down unblemished fruit,
which I scoop up, tear open,
and devour. He eats his share
before descending.
A coconut upon the ground
has split and lost its milk
but is easy to pry open with my knife.
I shake away the ants inside
and carve dry pieces
for the boy and me.
The sun is still so hot
that darkness will be long in coming.
There is, however, such a mossy place here,
it cannot hurt to lie upon it
for a while. Before
I turn to say this to the boy,
I am asleep.
I do not dream.

When I awake
the arms of manchineel trees
twist across the darkened sky.
I look first for the boy
in what is left of twilight
but see nothing moving,
not even a short shadow
that the moon might frame.
"Boy," I call, wishing
I had thought to ask his name.

"Boy?"

There is no answer.

I am once again

entirely alone.

Where is this glade? What is beyond?

Was this the destination in his mind?

Was he another emissary

of Aunt Margaret, as it seemed?

I am as wide awake

as I have been since I first ran.

It feels like the midpoint of night

or sometime just before,

a perfect time to travel, as Aunt Margaret said.

Yet travel where? I hoped for clues

from the uncommon boy.

My armpits are as sore now as my feet

and yet I cannot think

of pain or tiredness or fear.

With every step, I think of being

closer to a safer place. How

I will find it is unclear.

I have either missed the place I seek entirely

or it is very near. The island is not wide

but long. I feel as if I've walked the length

of it, for traveling across would not have

taken me so many days. The location

of the rising moon confirms this,

and I steel myself to push

through what remains

of trees and forest growth.
Head down, I start to run. But
all at once, so soon
it has the feeling of a dream,
there is a break within the trees
and then, beyond, a field
as open to the sky
as any I have passed through.
In the middle is a monstrous object, dark and solid,
indistinct. I do not dare approach it until morning.
I sit upon the ground, pull my knees
up to my chest, and wait.
I wait
the very darkest
hours of the night.
A soft rain seeps
into the canopy of leaves.
It drips along my shoulders
and bare arms as if I am a stone
and freshens all the sleepless hours.

19

Just before dawn
the contours of the object
are completely indistinct,
obscured by patches of thin fog. Then,
gradually, a haze falls over everything,
a soft sheen settles on the edges
molded by what light there is,
and colors, greens and grays
and pinkish tints like those
along the salt pond shore, begin
to make the form of it more clear
until it is so like the pictures
of the aeroplanes within my book
I half expect that it will rise.
In the full light of day, however,
I can see that it is rustier
than when Ashani brought me here,
and that it almost grows in place,
held down by vines
which travel in and over it,
surrounded by small clinging bushes
and tall weeds bent by pressure of its wings.
Wild frangipani saplings bloom at either end
and decorate it just as if it were
a crypt above the ground,

like those outside the village
that are placed to face the sea.
How is it possible my thoughts
had made this very battered thing
into a shining iron bird to lift me
from the island? Ashani
must have also held such thoughts
for him to signal me to meet him here.
Or did I really see the waving of his hand
in evening light? Did I imagine that
and the small paper plane as well?
Exhaustion floods me like a fever.
I drop upon the stony ground beneath the wings,
but though my eyes, my limbs, my head
are far too heavy to continue on, I cannot sleep.
There is a conversation in my head,
between two voices.
The first exclaims,
"He is not here!"
The second answers,
"But he soon will come!"
By afternoon there are small painful blisters
forming on my shoulders and my arms.
They sting like insect bites. At first
I cannot imagine what would make them form.
But glancing back I see the manchineels
and know that I have done a stupid thing
in sitting underneath their cover while
the rain washed poison sap upon me.

Overcome with misery,
I crawl within the shadow of a wing,
into the coolest, driest part, and doze.
Each time I open up my eyes
I think that I will find Ashani
grinning down at me.
Once a passing cloud mass
makes me sure his form
is holding back the sun.
Had I the strength,
I would jump up
for joy. The disappointment
following is like a lunge
at something in my gut.
When sleep at last arrives
I follow it
as deeply as it leads.

I do not know if days pass in this way
or if it is the drops of rain upon my face
that make me stir. I move to where
it washes over me and curve my tongue
to cup the moisture. Blessedly,
it also calms my blistered limbs.
Looking at the hard gray sky
I cannot sense the time of day.
I only know
it is not night and I am still alone.
No blue snakes,

no path of blue-eyed flowers,
no small boy.
No place to go.
What was I thinking when I ran?
It might have made more sense
to simply walk into the sea.
By now they must have found Aunt Margaret.
Ashani, too. And soon
they will find me.
I drink some water
but my stomach
knots again in fear.
I could eat nothing now,
even if full platters of all kinds of food
were once again
put down before me.
Beneath the rain's cold tears
I try to stand as if I were a tree.
That Ossada has abandoned me
is not surprising.
I am her disobedient child.
The only prayer I dare to utter
is a mystery to me.
Who is this *Lord* to whom
I find myself
still offering thanks
for being *wonderfully made*?

20

Sometimes I am certain that I hear
Ashani's voice or Margaret's.
I even think I see thin wispy
shapes of them that drift
between the plane and trees.
But when I call,
it is my own voice echoing
against the silence.
At one point I am sure I see
the foggy forms of ladies in their flying suits
rise from the ground like heat,
their long scarves blowing all about.
Soon my water skin
will be completely dry,
but I cannot leave here
to go in search of food
or drink or anything.
Two frogs jump down
from what must be their home
within the seat behind the wings.
I have heard them croaking there
and love these signs of life.
And yet they leap across me
just as if I am a thing
as lifeless as their home.

As the sun moves,
I drag myself
to keep within the shade.
The walk back to the trees
looms like a distance
greater than the sum of all the ones
that I have crossed already.
I have a little memory
of the day the English left.
I was so young Aunt Margaret carried me,
but she put me down
so she could hug the ladies one by one
in their long dresses. All
the ladies, Margaret
and the other women,
wept. The thinnest, tallest
lemon-smelling one
stooped down to stroke my cheek,
then turned to step into a fishing boat
while we just stood and watched
as they were carried by the oarsman
to a vessel at the silver line.
Where
did they go? Where
were they, men and women both,
taken on the shining ship?
Aunt Margaret said it was to some place
known as England, far away.
How did the vessel know

to come for them? Could
such a vessel come for me?
There is a book
Aunt Margaret showed me once,
with pictures of the shapes of other places
on the earth. Upon its pages,
great and craggy islands
float upon blue sea,
just like our tiny nameless home,
which is too small to picture.
She told me that the English
who had lived among us
returned across the widest part of blue
to a large island that was once their home.
My thought of home
has changed, as if
wild animals had torn the hearth
and living organs of it all apart
and savaged everything inside.
Can such a home be pieced together
like a mended basket of unnumbered reeds?
If I could now return and things could be
exactly as before, would I be satisfied?
Though I have escaped Nanina's knife,
another gash has opened
in the center of myself.
The farther that I travel
from the things I know,
the more I am certain

I can only mend
this widening wound
by moving on
to things I have not known.
I doze and wake so many times
my dreams reach over what is real,
the real becomes my dreams.
When voices enter them
they wash into my mind
like light and dark across my eyes.
One voice begins to penetrate the haze
and peals into my sleep—
just like the bells
the English rang to mark the hours—
until I force both lids to open,
my two eyes to make connections
in my mind to what I see.
For minutes I can't speak at all.
My mouth feels full of feathers,
and the words that slowly come
as thick as the soft down
beneath a duck.
The hands upon my blistered, bleeding ones
are firm and warm. They pull
until I stand and sway,
until I find that I am propped
against Ashani's solid form.
His smile is stretched
across such sadness in his face.

As he bends down to me
he holds his water skin up to my mouth
and does not talk until
I have had my fill.
"You took so long," he says at last.
But I protest: "You were
not there to show the way."
I have a sudden longing
for his arms to hold me up,
but he is treating me as if
I am an object made of glass.
He only says, "You should
have listened when I did."
I know Ashani's scolding well
and that it covers his concern.
"Where were you, then?" I say.
"When I came here
there was no sign of you."
"Helen. I waited here for days and days,
until it seemed that Esenu or someone else
had captured you. I did not learn
until I went back to the village
that he had failed."
"Aunt Margaret? Did they find my aunt?"
"They searched her hut, but only
when they thought that they would find you there."
I have not seen the place
where Aunt Margaret lives, so far
from all the others of our tribe.

How could I go there by myself?
Without Ashani I would be uncertain of the way.
Where is Aunt Margaret, now?
"Your mother worries you have starved.
I feared some kind of accident, a fall,
a poison plant."
"You taught me what is edible
and what is not,
and how to hide myself."
"I also taught you to avoid the manchineels
and where to find the plane,
but you forgot them both."
"Those are such different things. You led.
I followed."
"And so the fault is mine?"
"I never thought that I
would need to come here all alone.
And now I realize
what I believed could rescue me
is just a rusty, useless thing
that cannot take a flea into the sky."
Ashani laughs. "You saw it
with the eyes of your imagining.
It always was a wreck.
And how would either of us
know the way to lift
this heavy bird into the air?"
"I thought that you would know.
You said so many times

that you would learn."

Again Ashani laughs.

This time he cannot stop.

"Oh, Helen. All that I know,

I have learned upon this island.

The metal bird has come here from another world."

"Aunt Margaret says that there is one world only.

I have seen pictures of some other islands in it.

A few, she says, are called

by the name of *continent*."

"If she is right, how will we find such lands?

Who living there would take us in?"

I try to think of the unknown.

It is like reaching

for a misty shape suspended in the dark.

"I cannot go back," I say at last.

"I know," he answers me.

But does Ashani know the reason why?

My instincts
telling me that we are close upon
the far end of the island
have proved true. Already
I can smell the cliffs and egg rocks
where we used to come
in old Mototo's boat
to search the nests
of red-billed tropicbirds.
The salty henhouse smell
is unmistakable and strong.
"You are right," Ashani tells me.
"Do you have the strength to walk there?"
I try to stand up on my own but feel
my eyes begin to float out of my head
and swirl so that I have to sit down hard.
"Wait here," he says as if he thinks it possible
for me to just get up and walk away.
He runs back to the trees and soon returns
with mangoes in his hands. The firm, sweet fruit
revives us both a little, though I am still weak.
After a while I try to stand, and my two eyes
stay firmly in my head,
my knees begin to wobble less.
Ashani holds one arm

as if he thinks that I will fall.
When I do not
he puts my hand in his. Soon
turquoise ocean through the trees
is visible, and we begin to run.
As we come close, the birds
burst out like dark seaspray above the cliffs.
Out and back they fly
in wheels above the water
until the air is thick with feathered bodies;
others perch upon the rocks in restless groups.
From where we stand and look,
it is a great drop to the sea below.
We both bend down and lie upon our stomachs
at the edge, but not before the red bills sense us here
and raise a cry. Ashani points to something
far below, so far away I need to make slits of my eyes.
It seems to be a boat but is much the same color as the cliffs;
sometimes I make it out, sometimes the outline
is unclear. There are bright spots of color, though,
that separate and move about.
"Thanks to Hamani! They are here again,
 just as I thought," Ashani says.
"The scientists?" I ask.
"Yes. The ones who come here
 at this time of year
 to study nesting sites of tropicbirds."
"Before, I never showed myself until they left.
 I never spoke to one or saw beneath their hats."

"You have observed their boat is not as large as those
 that come from time to time to take the salt."
"Would they take me upon this boat?"
"Us," Ashani says. "For I am leaving, too.
I know the custom that you fear.
It is a bad thing. And the rule that
says the women may not learn to read.
That rule is bad as well. I do not want
the woman that I marry
to be scarred and without education too,
whoever she turns out to be."
Until the words he added at the last,
I thought he spoke of me.
But he is far from marriageable age himself.
I am astonished that he thinks into the future
in this way and is so ready to abandon
everything he knows. It is a desperate choice
for each of us, and one, I think,
that may not come to pass.
Surviving all alone so long
has made me love the island more
and want to leave it less.
"How can those people down below
see us up here?" I ask. "Why would they
take us, perfect strangers, on their boat?"
"Have you another plan?"
The plan I had was foolish,
and Ashani knows
that I have nothing else to take its place.

But his plan seems impossible as well.

The colorful and tiny people

scattered through the rocks

cannot climb up as high as we are,

and each head is looking down.

How will they ever see us on this edge?

How can we scale the jagged cliffs

down to their boat?

Ashani throws a stone

to watch it bounce from ledge to ledge.

"It might hit someone on the head," I say,

"or cause a red-billed tropicbird to leave its nest,"

which it is doing now upon each ledge it hits.

As each bird squawks, Ashani smiles.

The clatter of the stone soon dies

while it continues in its bounce and fall,

as if he'd thrown a ball of down.

"There is a path," Ashani says at last,

"some distance from this spot.

It comes out farther down the cliff

and is a place from which I have made my way

up to the nests before."

I feel a mix of hope and sudden fear.

"I cannot climb there yet. Just walking

from the plane was hard."

I think of slipping on a ledge,

all covered in the dung of birds,

and falling like the stone Ashani threw,

bouncing ledge to ledge

right to the sea and rocks below.
Ashani does not answer right away.
This is his way when contemplating
what to do. He starts to throw another stone,
but I reach up and grab his arm and pull it down.
"You are much stronger than you think," he says,
His happy mood begins to change.
"And yet, if what you say is true,
if you would be afraid to climb,
we will have to hide again.
The searchers will most surely
find us in this open place."
"But will not the people
soon get back into their boat and leave?"
"They might. Though
many times they stay for days.
We have to hope they just arrived."
More nights in tamarind trees do not appeal to me.
But it is clear Ashani has a new idea,
for he begins to lead me now
along the cliff's rim.
We keep so close to it
that my head spins,
and my legs shake
like trembling saplings
in the wind.

The cave Ashani brings me to
has a hidden entrance in the hillside
where the ledges end and manchineel trees grow.
The cave is well disguised by vines and large hibiscus,
which we pull apart to enter
a most terrifying blackness.
Ashani tears the bushes back,
to let the light come in,
and I see that I have been here once before.
It is a large, round, cavern room
with drawings on the walls, in dark red stain,
of men and women hunting.
They leap from wall to wall as if for joy.
Ashani tells me as I gape at them,
"I will weave the bushes back
so it will look as if there is no entrance,
yet some light will still come in."
"Will not Esenu look here for us?"
Ashani shakes his head.
"These are the pictures of the past,
which our tribesmen do not want to know about,
so no one speaks of them or comes here.
I found these long ago, by chance.
I think the only ones who
would remember they are here

are dead or much too old to know
the difference between dreams and what is real.
When, as a little child,
I told my father of the drawings,
he said that I was telling stories.
'Imagine,' he remarked to my two brothers,
'a frail woman hunting with a man!'
He cuffed me on the ear and laughed.
'How did such thoughts as these
take root in your young head?'"
The bodies in the drawings
are as naked as at birth.
In fact, they are the only truly
unclothed bodies of grown people
I have seen. They bound
so beautifully across the walls!
"Remember when you brought me here
and made me promise
not to tell about the pictures
to anyone—not even Suba?"
He nods.
"If we had lived so long ago," I say,
"we would not have to leave the island."
"But there were no things then called *books*," Ashani
teases me. "It is a futile exercise
to wish away the years."
I notice that there are no signs of animals about.
"Why do not cayawolves or lynx live in this cave?
Surely wild animals could make a home here."

"It is a sacred place," Ashani says. "An animal
knows where the spirits live and keeps away."
"And will the spirits mind that we are here?"
"I like to think that they
will understand and want to help us."
Sometimes I feel Ashani has a spirit in himself
that is quite old. And very wise.
I trust him more than anyone.
The cave is clean and dry,
as if it has been swept.
It smells of cassia flowers
and the fruit of calabash.
"I think Aunt Margaret has been here,"
I say, sniffing the air. "I am certain of it."
"Perhaps," Ashani says and smiles.
"But the scent in here is always like it is today,
as if this cave has been kept as a shrine."
"Such care would be
the kind of thing that she would take."
I want to think that she is near again
and knows that I am here this moment in this place.
"Perhaps she goes to hide here from my father
when he threatens her."
After the boy left,
was I supposed to find it by myself,
for surely Margaret knew
I could not fly away as I had thought?
It does not matter.
I am here and will be safe awhile.

I lie upon the smooth clean floor
and watch the figures
leaping through the air
until they disappear
in layers of deep sleep.

When I awake
I have the sense
of having slept a long, long time.
Ashani squats across from me
in front of piles of berries,
coconuts, and other things grown wild.
He gives me my full water skin and handfuls
of delicious nuts I have not tasted anywhere before.
This is so like the offerings within the fattening hut
that I begin to laugh until soon he is laughing, too.
"This time you need to eat to have the strength
for climbing cliffs—not to attract a husband."
I take small bites of almost everything,
eat three kumquats
and an entire pineapple myself.
"You slept so long," he says,
"I had to fill my time with things
like scaling trees and gathering nuts."
"How long? What day is this?"
"One day. One night."
"And you. Did you not sleep at all?"
"I slept at night, as normal people do.
Perhaps you would like this cave to be your home,

and for me to carry food to you each day until
you are as fat as any lady that we know."
I jump up flailing with my fists.
He grabs them one by one
and holds them tightly in his own.
"You know I needed rest," I cry.
"And you have had it. The scientists
are still upon the cliffs,
but they will leave before too long.
There is no time to waste."

We move most cautiously
into the narrow entrance to the cave,
spending the time to weave
the growth across it skillfully
before we start off for the cliffs again.
We have only gone a little ways
when Ashani stops and cocks his head
just like an animal who listens
to a sound not heard by human ears.
His eyes are closed, yet
he is more awake than ever,
speaking softly in a voice
I do not question.
"Our tribesmen are not far from here."
"Esenu and Dar?" I whisper.
"A greater number, an entire
tribal pod of them, I think."
We go back quickly to the cave,
and unfasten all the vines and limbs
so we may enter once again.
This time Ashani weaves the branches tightly
until there is no opening at all.
We sit once more upon the cold floor of the cave
in dark so black we cannot see each other's eyes.
For such an endless space of time

it is so still and quiet
I wonder if Ashani can be right.
Perhaps the men have turned
and are already on their way
back to the village.
But then Ashani starts to stiffen,
and in only minutes more we both begin
to feel the pounding throb
of many feet right through our skin.
They are so close their voices carry
through the cave and rumble
indistinctly in our ears.
Ashani puts his finger to my lips.
It is not necessary, for I am
much too afraid to speak.
It is clear that they are searching
for the very place in which we sit.
In their attempts to find the opening
they sometimes come dangerously close.
I calm myself
by thinking that because
the men have shunned this place for years,
it is just as Ashani says
and they will not know where to look.
With many searching, though,
it is quite possible that one
will stumble on our hiding spot,
and in the blackened silence
I can feel Ashani's fear

mixed with my own. Sometimes
we hear a rustling that is indistinct;
two or three times it seems as if the vines
across the door are being pulled apart,
and we cover up our ears
and huddle like some hunted things,
which I sometimes forget we truly are.
When not a slit of light breaks through
and all the tearing, swishing sounds
begin to fade, until
no sound at all is heard,
we uncurl and stretch our bodies,
but do not trust
that we can leave again for hours more.
It is so dark my eyes seem closed,
but all the while we stay in here
they are as open as two windows
with no cloth to cover them.

It has been quiet for
at least the space that would be morning,
and I beseech Ashani
that we try again to make our way
out to the cliffs, reminding him
the scientists may leave.
This time we are more cautious
as we go, alert for any noise
that is not made by animal or bird.
Ashani once again weaves carefully

until the entrance to the cave cannot be seen.
This little forest ends before the cliffs are reached.
Just as we leave the safety of its cover,
we see our tribesmen spaced along the edge,
set apart like brightly painted totems.
Some carry bows, some spears.
They all gaze down as if they mean
to frighten all the scientists away,
who cannot know it is not birders that our tribesmen seek.
We climb a large mahogany
where we can hide
but still observe these fierce, confused men.
For a long while they merely stand and stare.
But then a small explosion sounds,
from something that Ashani calls a *gun*.
The noise comes from below the cliff,
and all the searchers raise their hands
in hurried signals meaning *peace*.
But will those strangers understand?
More shots cause such a swift retreat
the men dart raggedly about
until there is no group at all
but only single warriors
dispersed in all directions.
When we have seen the backside
of the last, we take
our chance and shimmy down.
They will return,
and we can not be certain

of how large a space of time
or little while we have
before they can regroup
and come in search of us again.
We slip out from our hiding place
as swiftly and as silently as eels.

24

The path begins below the cave
and winds along some barren rocky ground
where a few scrawny frangipani
trees seek to survive. It cleaves
straight down against the rugged hillside
bordering the cliffs
and seems almost as treacherous
as the steep route along the ledges.
There are no places, though, that are impassable,
and we begin a steady, slow descent.
Below, the people are indeed
still scattered through the craggy bluffs,
still bent above painstaking work,
whatever it may be. We used to simply watch
the tropicbirds nest with their young,
but these observers
carry paper pads which they make marks upon.
My feet are hard and callused
yet the path is rougher than the forest floor,
with sharp stone places.
Ashani doesn't flinch,
but I step carefully.
It makes the going slow,
and he begins to hurry me.
For some time I keep up with him,

but then I stumble and fall hard upon a jagged place
and split my knee. Ashani's anger at himself
is fierce. I have not seen him so.
Yet he is gentle as he pours
cool water on the cut
and binds it with a strip of cloth
we tear from my danabo.
"We cannot stop here," he says
and then asks, "Can you go on?"
There is no shade. No covering at all.
What is my choice? My leg throbs
as I try to put more weight upon it;
Ashani glances nervously
at the few scientists
who are still on the cliffs.
As we descend, they grow
close enough for us to see
their features and the gestures that they make.
Some mouths are moving,
but we cannot hear the words they speak
in the distance and amid the cries of birds.
A number of the people have climbed
back into the boat. My heart
begins to beat into my throat.
"Are they about to leave?" I ask.
"I do not know," Ashani says.
"Perhaps they rest there
in the heat of noon."
"How will they see that we are here?"

"As we cannot hear voices,
they must be unable to hear ours as well.
Our calls would only float out to the sea."
This downward climb is painful. I simply put
one foot before the next and concentrate upon
Ashani's back. From time to time
we each look down and watch the people
as they stop their work. Soon
there is not one person on the cliffs
but many in the large and rocking boat.
Then all at once we hear a noise
that rips the air with growling sounds
and causes all the birds to rise at once.
Ashani shouts at me,
"They've started up their motor.
It is this engine that will carry them away.
They will never hear us now."
I do not know of motors.
Can they be the small gyrating things
I read about
that sit within the planes?
But there is clearly no more time.
The piece of cloth that binds my knee
is soaked with blood.
I tear it off and wave it, streaming red
into the wind. I wave and scream.
I scream until my voice gives out,
until Ashani's louder screams join mine.
What can we hope for,

high above the motor's noise?
Who has the ears to hear
our hoarse, weak cries?
At this same moment
clouds are passing
right across the sun.
Two people on the boat below
look up into the sky at the same time.
The shout of one is like a hiccup of a screech
but just enough to make the whole group
raise their eyes. One man
takes out the thing Ashani tells me
made the small explosions,
but another wrestles it away from him.
The motor stops,
and a shrill woman's voice
drifts up to us. "Don't shoot.
They are just children.
A young girl and a native boy!"
"Why would they shoot at us?"
I ask Ashani.
Ashani shakes his head.
"Perhaps they think
we are some stragglers from the tribe
and mean them harm."
Now they have seen us,
I quickly wrap the wound again
and press against the flow.
"Stay here," Ashani tells me. "I can

get there faster by myself."
I do not wish to be left all alone.
I argue that I will try to hurry,
though I know
it is impossible.
Ashani must ask all our questions,
and I wonder, could I,
like him, be brave enough to face
these strangers by myself?
I stand and watch him make his way
down to the place beside the cliffs
where he can cross and then descend.
Although he scuttles like a goat
it seems to be an endless trip.
When he emerges near the boat
and disappears inside it,
I drop down and start
to claw the ground beside me
with my nails. It seems
the space of one entire afternoon
before I see him once again upon the deck.
And then he climbs the cliff
and crosses to the path, and though
it feels like hours more before
he reaches me, I know that he is on his way.
The boat stays anchored.
The people stare straight up at me.
What have they told Ashani?

If they have agreed to take us with them,
where will the destination be?

He is not running
as he makes his way toward me
around a clump of mangroves.
I cannot read the answer on his face
until he is beside me and I see
the wet lines underneath his eyes,
thin streaks that tears make.
"They will not let us come," he says,
 not looking down.
"What did they say?"
"They said they cannot steal
 the children of this island."
"Did you not tell them
 the real reason we must leave?"
"I had no words for it."
 No words.
 I have the words,
 but is there any way for me
 to utter what I know?

25

"How many women are there on the boat?" I ask Ashani.
"I do not know. A few.
  They dress exactly like the men,
  in trousers and round hats."
  The motor is still quiet.
"I must go there," I say, rising.
"I must go there now."
"No. The path gets rockier
  closer to the sea."
"I will not fall again."
"You might."
"I will not!"
  He hands me my worn water skin.
"Carry this.
  It will take longer than you think."

The pain shoots almost to my ears as I begin,
but after many steps there is a numbing
from the motion of my feet. Ashani
was right about the path.
Halfway down,
it is not to be found.
The land becomes more barren
toward the sea, and at the place
where I can cross onto the cliffs

it blends into another chunk of ledge.
Here my feet begin to hurt as much
as my scraped knee. The blood upon the rock
is coming from small slashes
on their soles.
At times I look down
at the anxious faces of the people,
who look up as if they think
at any moment I may fall.
I dare not glance back at Ashani's face,
because the fear within his eyes
would be enough to cause my feet to slip.
There is the feeling I have had before
of time let loose,
as if this journey
has no starting place or end,
as if this downward trip will last a lifetime,
and the pain will never stop.
Arriving at the cliff
above the anchored boat,
I see no way
to get myself upon its deck.
Then two men stretch a blanket
and they yell for me to jump into it.
I hesitate, shut my eyes and leap.
The jarring catch
shoots pain into
the places it was not before.
It takes just seconds,

and in seconds more
I'm wrapped within the blanket
and am drinking bitter tea.
"Did not your friend convey our message?"
says one lady, who has spectacles
pushed up into her hair of straw.
"Did you not understand?"
"I understand," I say.
A bearded man appears
and tells me how
they make a policy
of never taking island children from their home.
"We come here only for the birds," another lady says.
Her skin is pale but splotched with brown.
"I understand," I say and wait
while they exchange queer private looks.
"But you do not."
"Come now," the one with spectacles exclaims,
"it's clear you want to run away from home,
as many children do from time to time."
She tells me that they live across the sea,
on an island known as England,
and that we would find it strange.
"There'd be no going back."
"I understand," I say.
The woman wipes her brow and smiles.
"But you do not," I say.
The splotchy lady tells the others
I am merely frightened and confused.

Then she turns back to me and asks,
"What is it that you really want?"
I do not know the way
to tell them what I must.
"It's clear enough. They're runaways,"
the lady with the spectacles proclaims.
"We run away," I say. "That is quite true."
"Just as we thought!"
But I go on. "We run away
from something that makes it impossible to stay."
Afterward, the words I wish to use
become like stones within my mouth,
for it appears I have said something
that they did not wish to hear.
When I sputter that I cannot
speak the things I need to say
before so large a group,
the blotchy lady
tells the others to go
"down below."
A small man with a tiny voice
objects and says that it is time to leave.
"The weather's fair, the tide's just right.
What if those men with spears return?"
But no one listens, and they move inside.
In all the quiet left behind
I think of how
I am not used to speaking
to a woman quite as pale as this one,

whose blood must not run red.

But there is no one else to tell my story to.

However difficult, I have to try.

"There is a ceremony," I begin

and then describe, the only way I can,

the painful things that I have learned.

When I have finished, she is white

beneath the brownish spots.

She puts her hand up to her mouth.

"It cannot be!"

"It happens in this way to every girl here.

It would have happened so to me."

I pause. "And that is why I ran away."

Her eyes are wide. She does not move.

"I've never heard of such a thing!"

I show my knee, my bleeding feet,

the blisters on my back and arms,

my scratched and sunburned face.

I look down at the scabs upon my hands.

"These things I suffered in an effort

to escape the truth of what I tell."

She remains quiet and stays seated for a while.

When she can speak again,

her words catch in her throat.

She strokes my hair.

"You are so very young."

Then she gets up and

tells me to stay where I am.

Inside the cabin

there is silence when she enters,
but in time I hear
one of the others say, "My God!"
And then some mumbling sounds.
When they begin to come back on the deck,
their eyes are turned away from me. Only
the lady that I told drifts over, looking stern
but softened in a most peculiar way.
"We have agreed. It is *asylum* that you seek.
Can you remember that? You cannot merely say
to the authorities that you have run away."
"What is this word?"
"*Asylum* is safe harbor.
Yes. That is exactly what it is.
A place where you won't be afraid."
I must inquire, "What of Ashani?"
She looks confused. "The boy?
I do not know about the boy."
"He hates these practices," I say,
"and does not want a wife so scarred."
There is a second meeting,
but it does not last as long.
When they return, this lady says,
"I'm sorry. We must leave the boy behind."

26

"You cannot!" I implore.
But they are firm in what they
have agreed must be.
I do not hesitate:
"Then I myself will stay."
The lady starts to roll her watery eyes
shot through with tiny lines of red.
"Wait just a moment more."
She calls another meeting,
and I cannot hear a thing they say.
There is much head-shaking.
When she returns, the answer
is not on her face.
But then she says,
"It is decided. He may come,
but he will need to work for his passage."
A shriek I did not know
was waiting in my throat
escapes my mouth.
I stand to wave both arms
and beckon Ashani. At first
he does not stir, but then
his sprint along the path
seems blown by unseen wind.
When he arrives I see

that he has brought the things we had with us.
"Is this all that you own?"
the straw-haired lady asks us twice,
examining my books, our water skins,
the knives that we both carry.
I feel ashamed to own so little
in her eyes. Ashani nods.
He has not spoken once
since he jumped down upon the deck.
The bearded man is pacing back and forth.
"There's no more time to lose," he says at last.
He gives Ashani something very like
the shirt he wears himself. One lady
pulls a loose dress over me.
It binds my arms and is too stiff.
The motor has begun again
and sounds much louder
now that we are close to it.
The boat begins to back away
from the cliffs. Until this moment,
I have been too centered on our fear,
and on our awful need to beg for help,
to think of what we leave.
But looking at the cliffs, the violet sky
all flocked with clouds,
the spindly mangroves clinging to the rock,
I am besieged by all the beauty of our island,
even this small piece of it. My mind
floods with clear pictures

of the places I have passed through,
of the village and the airy houses
slung between the trees
that we have lived in all our lives,
of our good large mother
and my brothers, tall and powerful and kind,
of Suba—sweet and trusting Suba.
And of Margaret. My Aunt Margaret,
who has given me the vision to believe
that I may choose what I will do,
and honor who I am.
Will she be lost to me as well?
"Look," Ashani says.
He points up to the path along the cliffs,
where two small figures make their way
in our most recent footsteps.
At first I think they must be
tribesmen, that they have
come back just in time
to block our escape. But then
I see that these are female travelers.
One wears a colorful danabo, one a head cloth
the deep color of the sea.
Ashani's quick and searching eyes
inform him sooner
than my own can tell me what I see.
"It is your sister Suba and your aunt!"
The two both wave their arms about
as we did only hours earlier.

"Stop," I shout and run to warn
  the man within the wheelhouse.
"What is it now?" he says.
  I wail, "It is my sister Suba on the path.
  She is a young girl, too. We cannot leave her here."
  Aunt Margaret must have warned her
  and then helped her get away,
  or she would not be out here now.
"Oh, please," I beg. "Do not abandon her."
"Go back," the lady with the spectacles
  begins to yell,
  and I think it is at Suba
  but it is instead
  at the same agitated man.
  He is red faced
  but takes the boat a second time
  to where it first was anchored.
  We wait again,
  and he drums callused fingers on the wheel,
  but it is not so very long
  before my sister hesitantly
  separates from Margaret
  and then crosses just as we did
  to the outcroppings above us.
  Suba jumps, and soon I hold
  her wonderful, lithe body
  in my arms. Then I wave to beckon Margaret,
  but she stops along the path and nods
  as if to say, "I need to stay."

"What will she do?" I ask Ashani.

"What she has always done," he answers.

"We may not be the first
    to leave the island with her help,
    and we will probably not be the last."

Suba is crying. The truth
    about the hut and ceremony,
    the idea of leaving here, are both so new.

I hold onto her as tightly as I can,
    and grasp Ashani's hand.

The scientists are quiet now, or muttering,
    and some have gone below.

The boat stays idling by the cliff
    for such a long while that I am confused.

They were in such a hurry earlier to leave.

I am surprised to see, at last,
    the solemn, bearded one approaching us.

He clears his throat.

"I'm truly sorry," he begins, "but you
    must make a choice. We cannot
    take all three of you."

I feel my stomach lurch and sink.

I pull my sister Suba close.

"You told us," I protest.

"But I was wrong. Besides the fact that
    there just isn't room, the boy will not
    be able to request asylum, as we said. There
    is no present threat to him."

He points at Suba.

"If *she* had not appeared,
  we might have taken that slim chance."
"But now?"
"The boy should stay."
  Leave Ashani here! The thought is like
  a sudden firestorm. Earlier
  I did not hesitate to say I could not
  leave my friend behind. But now,
  with Suba here, with what we both,
  as females, will find waiting
  for us if we do return,
  my thoughts are painful and quite clear.
  Ashani quickly pulls
  the shirt he wears over his head,
  throws it down upon the deck,
  climbs up the ladder,
  and then scrambles to the cliff.
  I do not try to hold him back.
  With his feet planted firmly on the rock,
  he looks at me in such a wrenching way.
  There is both challenge there
  and lingering sadness wrapped in one.
  His words surround me like a breaking wave:
"You must explore this island that you travel to
  without me this one time."
  He almost smiles. How can he smile?
"You must remember everything you find
  so you can one day show it all to me.
  There will be schools, Helen. Imagine. Schools!"

Schools. The word excites me even as I
feel a surge of loss that makes me
think I cannot stand. Leave Ashani?
Is such a thing a possibility?
How long before he follows?
Will he remember me?
A sob escapes me
like a sudden gasp for help.
Suba holds on to me
with trembling arms
and rests her head against my neck.
"Will we come back?" she says
as quietly as if she only breathed the words.
The boat begins to slowly back away.
A deep, hard ache is pressing
just behind my eyes,
but I seek Ashani's fast-receding shape,
and the tiny figure of Aunt Margaret on the path,
as if to burn the images into my brain,
as if I cannot ever let
another image take their place.
And then, a short ways out,
so suddenly that I am wholly unprepared,
the vessel takes the island from me
with one turn and surge of power
in a flourish of white froth.
Above the glare
of sun upon a watery trough,
I fasten my blurred vision

on the silver line ahead
that seems to move away from us
as steadily as we proceed
through rocks and swirling surf
and make our way across
the beds of kelp and coral reef
until the only thing
ahead of us
is open sea.

Author's Note

I learned about "the fattening room" from an article in the *Boston Globe* that described it as a custom of some tribes in Nigeria who traditionally confine young women in a special room for weeks in order to fatten them up and make them more marriageable. The concept of beauty this encourages seems so antithetical to that of the typical American teen that I began thinking of ways to use it in a novel. When I looked for more information, it became clear that female circumcision was often an integral part of the fattening practice. I also learned that a moderate to radical form of this mutilating procedure is performed on millions of girls annually in about thirty countries throughout the world, even clandestinely in the United States. The various reasons given for this tradition are many and differ from country to country. Some tribes regard the practice as a rite of initiation into womanhood; others see it as a means of protecting virginity or removing what is considered by some cultures to be a male part of the female genitals. Where the practice exists, it usually reflects the sexual mores and superstitions of a male-dominated society and is paradoxically kept alive by the elder females.

The fattening room is a Nigerian custom, but since female circumcision is practiced throughout Africa, my reading began to include books set in different parts of this continent and written by both Africans and foreigners steeped in African cultures and customs. I was drawn to the stories of women who had left their tribes and country in order to escape a requirement that they had come to consider senseless and mutilating, or to seek medical treatment for the effects of the ritual genital cutting that had been performed on them as children or young teenagers. Some side effects can include not only difficulty with intercourse and childbirth but also problems with other bodily functions such as menstruation, urination, and defecation.

I was struck as well, by the view of the anthropologist Ellen Gruenbaum, in *The Female Circumcision Controversy,* that we can have little hope of the abandonment of this custom as long as a woman's marriageabilty and long-term security are dependent upon it. As in other areas, education and equal opportunity are keys to the process of change, and Ms. Gruenbaum sees this process beginning to happen in countries such as Sudan.

While doing the research for my novel, I quickly came to realize that I'd need to be grounded in both country and culture in order to write convincingly. When this didn't appear possible and I spoke of abandoning the project, a number of writer friends suggested I invent my own culture, customs, and rules. Intrigued by this advice, I placed the action of the novel on a mythical island and was so encouraged by my friends' reception of the first two chapters that I decided to continue developing the characters and situations. I crafted imaginary names for clothing and gods, and interspersed invented names for foods, plants, animals, and birds with real ones.

At about this same time, I came upon a map of Anguilla, an island in the British West Indies, that seemed very much like the island I had imagined. In order to learn more about Anguilla's history, culture, geography, topography, flora, and fauna, my husband and I made a trip there that proved to be invaluable.

The purported British influences on my mythical island helped me to determine the novel's "voice," which seemed to flow naturally. The first three chapters were originally written in prose, but then, because of the formal speech patterns of the characters, the narrative began setting itself up as a long poem.

I hope *The Fattening Hut* will be read as the mythic tale that I intended it to be. As with all myths, it is grounded in truth and presents ideas that are meant to resonate throughout the human community.